AF506660

The Time Hunter Tales:

 Mind Wanderer
 The Lost Finders
 Knight of the Wolves
 Storm from the Past
 New Tales of the Old World
 The Heroic Calamity
 To Void And Back

Poetry:

 Pathfinding

FANG Net

FANG Net

Evan A. Cushing

FANG Net

Published by Primordial Albion Press, 6 Albion Street, Salem, MA, USA

ISBN: 979-8-9873278-6-9 (paperback)
       979-8-9873278-7-6 (eBook)
Library of Congress Control Number: 2026905828

CONTENTS

Moving Parts

Jeff and Ruth's side

Jeff Fields got a call marked urgent from a number on his client list early one morning.

Jeff's heart shifted from power saving to standard power in a few seconds. Then the process to wake from sleep mode began. In another few seconds the extra filters in his lungs followed suit, then the kidneys, then the diagnostic algorithm in his brain implants double checked to make sure everything was bug free and fully functional. After that his brain jump-started and his eyes (the only obvious bionic part of his body) snapped open, seeing the call that had caused his sudden reboot hanging off to one side of his augmented vision. Jeff blink-clicked the message linking the call to his audio sensors as his brain's firewalls went up to full and his diagnostics into overdrive as they always did when accepting data from external sources.

"This is Fields. How can I help you?" Jeff subvocalized.

"Detective Fields, this is Officer Ruth Ranger. I'm a peace officer in distinct 5 of the LPD. Your grandfather was found dead this morning. I'm sorry for your loss. I was ordered to bring you over to your grandfather's home. How soon can you be ready?"

Jeff took a deep breath, calming himself and willing his adrenaline glands to not go into overdrive. "Give me half an hour, Officer Ranger. I'll meet you outside my residence."

"Very well. Thank you for your cooperation, Detective," Ruth replied.

"And Officer, I'm a private investigator. Just another civilian on Leviathan," Jeff added before the call disconnected.

"You took oaths almost as binding as mine but very well, I will see you outside your residence, investigator," Ruth replied matter-of-factly before cutting the call.

Jeff got up and pushed himself into the shower, allowing the skin-safe mist of dirt-eating chemicals to envelop him. Jeff took a long breath, trying to force his mind to analyze dispassionately without falling into sudden and unexpected grief at the death of his last family member and mentor. "Damn it all," Jeff thought, realizing he would not be able to be totally dispassionate or calm this day but knowing from his time teaching and researching bionic security as well as bio science that just being able to act with logic and remaining mostly calm was as close as he would get to being impassive.

Jeff got dressed quickly, downing some nutrient paste on his way out of his main-deck-level apartment on one of Earth's last few cities, all of which had begun life as interstellar colony ships.

Near the front door idled a patrol car with the peace officer at the wheel who turned to regard Jeff, who felt an IFF ping off his systems. The patrol car's passenger door swung open as Jeff approached. "Investigator," the officer said calmly.

Jeff nodded and got in the car which moved skillfully into the lanes for manual driving, avoiding all lanes earmarked for automated transit. Jeff found Officer Ranger a little odd. The officer wore an eyepatch over her right eye that did not fully hide a jagged and old scar. The officer wore a radio, had no visible cybernetics, and gave off no wireless signals of her own. There were only a few reasons someone would reach adulthood without any bionics being installed. Most were ideological in one form or another. A few religious sects were firmly opposed to physical enhancement. There were also a few rare physical and mental conditions that made physical enhancement very hard or even impossible.

Jeff had never met any emergency response personnel that had not been physically enhanced. The tests to qualify were brutal enough with extensive physical enhancement. Jeff felt his mind begin to analyze the officer instead of dwelling on the loss of his family.

"Something on my face?" Ruth asked sternly.

"You don't have any bionics, do you?" Jeff asked.

"Is that going to be a problem?" Ruth asked, a hint of anger coloring her tone.

Jeff knew he had let his curiosity get the better of him. "Not at all. I'm just surprised. You must be quite skilled."

Ruth was about to snap again but realized her passenger at least sounded sincere and civil, unlike nearly everyone else she had met on the job before they got to know her. "It's a hypersensitive immune system type: severe implant rejection. Let's leave it at that."

"Right. Sorry. I'm not usually this jumpy," Jeff apologized.

The trip to Jeff's family home was on the longer side. The home sat atop a landfill in the composting district. Wireless signals were spotty at best given the almost nonexistent signal boosters. They slipped from the city's main thoroughfare onto an old two-lane road.

The road was an oddity in a place where four lanes were usually the bare minimum, two for self-driving and two for manual. Eight lanes were standard for main roads, six for self-drive and two for manual.

Jeff looked up the man-made hill as they approached his oldest haunt. Three vans, five patrol cars, a sports car, and an old compact car from before self-drive was a thing all sat on the lawn. Jeff fell into his habit of analyzing before anything else. "That's a third of the local precinct, right?"

Ruth did some quick mental math, glad her charge was not a gibbering wreck like so many others she had seen in similar circumstances. "It's a fifth if you don't count the dispatch and office teams." Jeff took a deep breath. Ruth added, "We have a few minutes. You can take your time."

Jeff took a few more breaths, reconstructing his disconnected professional mindset. "Ok, lead the way," he said.

Ruth studied her charge for a few seconds then unlocked the car. "Ok, follow me."

Ruth led Jeff to the front door. Two peace officers who were clearly well over 50% enhanced, maybe even closer to

80%, stood by the door. Jeff felt the two officers scan him and Ruth before they stood aside.

Ruth led the way in. Another officer sat near the entrance watching those within the building. "Harold, which way's the chief?" Ruth asked the interior guard.

"The kitchen's still fuming over the lack of wi-fi," Harold said. He gave Jeff a once-over but soon switched focus back to the interior.

Ruth led the way to the kitchen. Jeff began to reminisce about the time spent running along the same route when he was younger and his parents were still around.

"You all right?" Ruth whispered.

Jeff shook off the lingering memories and redoubled his focus. He nodded and they continued in silence.

In the kitchen stood a team of technicians and a Detective Alexanderson who Jeff had worked with before on a few occasions.

"I understand the power fluctuations are an issue but we need those signal boosters set up ASAP," Alexanderson told the oldest technician.

"With all due respect, Detective, the power fluctuations are anomalous. Until we can find and isolate what's causing them it is unsafe for my crew to interface with the network any more than we already are," the old technician explained calmly, with the certainty of a man who had conversations just like this all his life.

"We need access to the precinct's resources. I can send runners for everything." Alexanderson grumbled.

"We are cut off from the network out here. Just give my team a few more hours. I'll make sure to complete a full report on the power fluctuations. If I were you, Detective, I'd investigate those after you talk with your guest, perhaps," the old technician replied.

Alexanderson turned around to find Jeff and Ruth looking at him. "That will be all, Sanders," the detective said, but the old technician had already slipped away to check over his crew's data.

"Fields, I need you to check your grandfather's computers. Tell me if there is anything odd or out of place," Alexanderson explained.

"Where is he?" Jeff asked.

"The body is on the way to the morgue for autopsy," Alexanderson replied.

Jeff took a deep breath. "Where was he found?"

"His lab, which is where I need you to go. Will that be an issue?" Alexanderson asked.

"No it won't. I need answers too," Jeff said.

They made their way to the lab, passing rooms where people checked the home's systems, searching for virus and data corruption. "You think something in the local network killed him?" Jeff realized.

"It's our best theory so far," Alexanderson nodded.

They arrived at a side room filled with a mainframe, desk, computer, slightly charred chair, and two walls of filing cabinets.

Jeff looked around the lab, closed his eyes, and took a few deep breaths. He was grateful the others gave him time to center himself. "Ok. I'm ready."

"Excellent," Alexanderson said before rolling a stool taken from another room over to the desk.

Jeff took a seat and slowly powered up the mainframe and computer. A prompt came up informing him the device had been partway through a debugging sequence before being shut down. From the prompt Jeff learned his grandfather had been debugging something on the ancient USB device plugged into the old school desktop computer and that the sequence had been cut off when the mainframe and desktop were forcibly shut down.

Jeff informed his companions about the facts before adding, "The USB in here is suspicious."

"Would restarting the sequence be dangerous?" Alexanderson asked.

"You don't know either, Detective?" Ruth could not help asking.

"I'm unfamiliar with tech this old. That USB likely predates the construction of our cities, let alone the wasteland," Alexanderson replied.

Jeff butted in before the conversation could derail. "Brute-forcing a shutdown is a serious emergency measure. Did you learn how the chair burned?"

"Electric overload. It looks like a botched intrusion into his neural network via hardware jack," Alexanderson explained.

"Wait, Gramps was plugged into his computer while running a debug script?" Jeff asked.

"That's right. Any idea when he got that USB?" Alexanderson replied.

"No idea. But if he ran tests on it before, I'm sure Gramps would have bragged about it. Working pre-collapse tech is rare. What bugs me is if he never tested it before, he would not have plugged himself into the network while it was there," Jeff said.

"That makes sense. We will have to look into this more. If you power the lab down again will the debug still be on hold?" Alexanderson asked. Jeff nodded. "Then shut it down like that," Alexanderson added.

"So what else do you need?" Jeff asked.

"You should go to the station. You will need to sign out the body. I'll get the estate and will documents forwarded to the precinct and reserve a room for you to use for the day. Officer Ranger, you are on escort detail for the day."

Ruth led her charge back to the car. Soon they were cruising back to the city proper. Jeff watched the sparse trees pass. Once they hit the main road Ruth let the car's auto-drive take over.

They watched as life continued as normal under the shade of skyscrapers packed like cigarettes in the decommissioned colony ship turned city-state.

The car turned off auto-drive as it pulled up to a security gate by the precinct.

Ruth rolled down her window and handed over an ID to the guard at the entrance to the precinct's staff parking, which was set below street level. Ruth and Jeff walked up a narrow stairway to the morgue.

The morgue's small waiting room was empty. No one was sitting behind the bulletproof reception window. Ruth hit a button, and a low chime sounded throughout the room. A few minutes later a man in a set of red scrubs walked to the window. "How can I help you?"

"We are here to see the body of Andrew Fields. The victim's family still needs to identify the deceased," Ruth explained.

The worker looked over a computer and turned the screen, showing an image of an old man's body lying on a plastic table. Jeff choked down his feelings. "That's my grandfather."

The morgue worker quickly turned the screen back and entered a note into the system. "Thank you for your assistance. Room 2m-2a has the other documents. The receptionist up there should be able to direct you where to hand them in afterwards."

Taking one of the elevators set between the morgue and staff parking, Ruth and Jeff arrived at the precinct's second above-deck floor. Both knew the precinct's main floor's layout. A few officers and office staff briefly greeted Jeff as he walked over to the administrative section and to room 2m-2a.

Ruth unlocked the door with her handprint. A tablet sat on the table. Jeff unlocked the tablet with his own fingerprint, which also read his DNA.

The files on the tablet were the last will and testament of Andrew Fields, an empty investigation report form, an NDA about the circumstances of Andrew Fields's death, and a paystub for services rendered thus far. Jeff rubbed his eyes. "This will take a while. Any chance I can get a coffee?"

Ruth smiled. "Sure." She went over to a panel on the wall and ordered two coffees and a small tray of muffins from the mess. She waited by the door while Jeff began to fill out his investigation report.

Soon a small robot pinged the door panel. Ruth took the tray from the bot and took the food over to Jeff while the bot went back to its duties.

The two humans sat in silence, both filling out reports and eating slowly in a meeting room that could comfortably house twenty people. Jeff enjoyed the stillness in the room, so at odds with the overpopulated hustle and bustle of Leviathan city.

Hours passed. The muffin tray was empty and coffee had been refilled three times when Jeff began to look over his grandfather's will. His grandfather's possessions went to Jeff, the money to Jeff's cousin Amellia Smyth. Andrew Fields's royalties and rights from inventions and discoveries would be shared between Amellia and Jeff.

Amellia lived on Behemoth, another one of the five city-states. Those five city-states were the only population centers left on Earth, though Behemoth was on the other end of the world. Amellia was a biotech specialist who was one of those creatives who would hyperfocus on a task, only sleeping when on the brink of collapse, so it was hard to predict when she would reach out to him or if his calls or emails would be looked at any time soon. Jeff set an alarm midday the next day to remind him to call Amellia.

Many hours later Jeff had finished his work. "Ok, I'm all set," he said as he stood up stretching.

Ruth looked up from her own tablet where she had been keeping track of Alexanderson's investigation and keeping an eye on the news while checking in with reports about Jeff's safety every hour.

"Ok. Receptionist first?" Ruth asked.

Jeff nodded slowly, having forgotten about seeing the receptionist. "That's right."

Second floor reception was by the main elevators between the administrative offices, dispatch section, and evidence storage.

"Hello Mr. Fields. I believe you have something for me," a large muscular receptionist said jovially.

Jeff grinned and handed over the work tablet. "Yuri! It's been a while."

"Only a few weeks. I found a new restaurant. Amazing spare ribs and burgers. We should go sometime with some of the old college crew." Yuri smiled easily, gently taking the tablet.

"Do they have any vegan stuff? You know, if we bring the crew we need to make sure Amanda, Jean, Clowe, and Francis can eat," Jeff asked.

"Who do you think I am? Of course they do." Yuri laughed before handing Jeff a tablet with a money transfer form. "Looks like you have a bonus."

Jeff looked the form, signed it and handed it back. "Ok. I'll be in touch. That all you need from me?"

Yuri glanced at the form and waved. "No, that's it. Stay in touch, my friend."

"Sure, Yuri. See you around," Jeff replied before turning to Ruth. "That's all I needed."

"Ok. I'll drive you back to your place, all right?" Ruth asked.

Jeff took a few deep breaths. "Thanks. I appreciate it."

The drive back was quiet. Around double the number of automated cars than normal were on the road.

Spanner in the Works

*R**uth's side**

Over the next few days the city's automation slowed down. Robots of all kinds lagged. IT departments across the city had not found the cause yet but it was becoming clear something was odd in the city's central networks.

Ruth was called in to check on a maintenance team. The team had been out of contact for a day, five levels under the main deck. It was rare for anyone to be this deep in the ship. The lack of good air, working water, and sporadic electrical levels made it difficult even for squatters to live this deep in the old beached ship.

A team of twelve officers had been called. Ruth was placed under command of Corporal Harold James (who Jeff would recognize as a door guard from his grandfather's home), who led six of the officers, including Ruth. Sargent Xex Primfell was leading the other six but was in charge of the entire team.

Xex was one of those officers who had over half his body replaced by cybernetics, signing away his life's service to the city in the process. The only ways out of this kind of employment were death, being too damaged to repair, or retirement at 60, though very few lasted that long.

The elevators only got the team to the third below-deck level before refusing to budge any further, making the officers take the maintenance stairs the rest of the way. The stairs were in poor repair but had been fixed many times. Even if the ship's hull and internal supports were the priority for maintenance crews, things like stars and elevators were still on the list of things to fix more often than not. The only other thing on the list of important repairs was the wi-fi network so messages could be sent around the old bulkheads and search crews would not need to be called in on the very delayed team.

The fifth under-deck level was hot, far hotter than it should be. Ruth squinted though her EVA suit's mask. This deep, a sealed suit providing a breathable atmosphere was a must. Lack of air was a hazard, as were extreme cold, ice, floods, and gas pockets. High heat was very, very odd in an unpowered area and could be extremely dangerous.

Xex pointed at two team members, one from each half of the unit. "Wi-fi's down. You and you, go up as may levels as you need and report on the environment. Anything new and myself or Corporal James will send a runner to update."

Ruth checked her wi-fi. Seeing it was fully cut off, she had no idea when this had happened but was glad her team leaders had spotted the issue and were working around it.

Xex continued to use his suit's external speakers instead of the radio. "All of you, make sure to keep an eye on the map of our search area. Do not go outside of it without my express approval and stay in sight of your team. Everything else, business as usual. No heroics. Just stay with your assigned team and be careful. Move out!"

The teams split as directed. Ruth took point because she did not have enhancements to rely on. She had trained herself to be the best of the best, earning the grudging respect of most of her colleagues.

Ruth, her head on a swivel, kept an eye on the suit's senses and the area all around her for clues and hazards. The team stayed close, sometimes sending two members down a short dead-end path while keeping eyes on each other.

It began to feel even hotter. Ruth could have sworn her suit's current temp had gone up even higher. She looked up her suit's temperature logs, finding a steady increase in heat. "Sir, the heat's rising."

Harold replied, "I know. Stop here." The team halted, making sure they had an unobstructed view of the ceiling and were not next to any scrap or low overhangs. "Two-minute break. Make sure you are hydrated." Harold altered his scanner from all around and low power to just in front of him with longer range and power. "The heat gets dangerous further down. Sounds like a fire. Decon, it's your turn to be the runner. Go and let anyone you meet know we are requesting backup."

After two minutes of rest, Officer Kat Decon bolted back the way they had come. Harold looked at his remaining three teammates. "Ok, the four of us will take a look. Stay close and make sure to keep track of the heat and sound."

A few passages later Ruth and company came upon a massive open room, far different from the passages where sometimes only three could walk abreast. A huge machine took up half the seemingly endless space. Worse, the contraption was on fire and charred bodies lay around it. Ruth took two steps into the room towards the nearest body when a hand gripped her shoulder. "Don't. They are gone. We'll wait for backup and gather as much data as we can from here." Harold's normally lazy voice was firm.

Ruth choked down an argument. She knew her team leader was objectively right but still she felt like waiting even a second was abandoning the dead team before her.

Three minutes of gathering data later, Harold fell to the ground, clutching his face. "Fuck. The static's getting worse."

"Sir?" Ruth asked.

"Cybernetics are acting up. The whole team was feeling it on deck three. Glad one of us is fine, at least," Harold explained, trying to keep some levity in his voice.

"Sir, do I need to carry you and Stevens back?" Ruth asked, now feeling more than a little annoyed at having been left out of that discussion.

"Sir, I think we should go back. The static's worse here," Greg Stevens said.

"Fine, fine. I swear Ruth, you will make captain someday," Harold said.

Ruth led her team back to where they had gotten their break. The going was slow. After five minutes of walking they came upon the rest of their twelve-officer team. "How bad?" Xex asked. His voice was filled with static and pain.

"Better than you, sir," Harold said though gritted teeth.

"Interference is rising," Greg explained.

"So is the heat. We go back to the stairway. Officer Ranger, fire control on the third level still works. Go there and do everything you can to flood this level," Xex said.

Ruth saluted her team. "Understood, sir. See you all soon." Then she sprinted as if her life depended on it, using her suit's backup battery to fuel the AC and scanner systems in her suit.

Ruth ran but the heat at her back kept rising. Her breath slowly became labored but she kept going. The walls boiled as she focused on just moving. Passing the elevator without a second thought, she bolted up the stairway.

The moment Ruth saw her wi-fi connect to the city's network she cried out on the emergency frequency, "This is Officer Ruth Ranger 5lpd-1196-49b. Discovered large scale fire on under-deck five. Maintenance team dead. Rest of my team are still moving up. I'm going to turn the pumps on under-deck three to flood deck five as ordered."

A few seconds ticked by but they felt like centuries. "Understood, Officer Ranger. Send data of the fire ASAP. We are routing fire teams in your direction." The response was professional and sounded less tense than Ruth, which was enough to help her calm down slightly.

Ruth sent all the data she had on the fire over the emergency line. That stressed her wi-fi connection but it held strong enough to keep the upload going, but only as long as she did not speak over the line.

She kept running. On under-deck three she saw a few squatters but ignored them as she ran past.

The pump room was rusted but the gauges and sensors still had power. Ruth plugged her suit's systems into the pump's main control. Her hands danced across a holographic keyboard projected in front of her as she took control of the pump.

The data upload finished just before Ruth reached the system. Her access to the voice systems was back. "Upload done. Flooding now." She called out on her team's and the emergency channel.

"Fire team ten minutes out. Who authorized the flood?" a voice replied over the emergency line.

"Sergeant Xex Primfell authorized that release. This is Corporal Harold James. Our team needs medical attention ASAP. We are by the deck three lifts," Harold called out.

"This is fire marshal Kaun, Sergeant Primfell. Please confirm," a new voice commanded.

"I'm declaring the sergeant MIA along with four other team members," Harold replied coldly.

In the next few seconds Ruth fully understood the term deafening silence.

"Understood. Help is on the way," Kaun replied.

Ruth raced to her team. She found them lying charred and broken. Ruth took out her medical kit which was only intended to treat one person's superficial wounds. "Treat yourself first, Ranger," Harold coughed from a wall he had propped himself up on.

"But sir," Ruth began.

"Nothing that kit can do for us," Harold replied. Ruth glanced at his helmet which lay partly melted on the ground next to him. Harold added, "It was a blow-up. We almost made it out before the wall of fire caught us. Seems to have died down for now."

Jeff's side

Jeff was lying in bed. His cousin was due to arrive in a few days. Jeff had taken a week off from teaching for bereavement purposes.

A new call came in from someone who always gave Jeff difficult jobs. "Clowe," Jeff said.

"Fields, I need your help once more," his oldest friend said.

"You wouldn't be asking unless this was serious. What's up?" Jeff asked, sighing internally.

"I'm asking as fire marshal Clowe Kaun. We had a fire on under-deck five. It's bad. An acquaintance of yours is being investigated for negligence. The thing is, I don't trust the police investigators to be impartial. I need your eyes on this, old friend."

Jeff sat up, rubbing his eyes. "Right. Where do you need me?"

"On under-deck three, northwest sector, by the main elevators. I'd understand if you refuse," Clowe said.

Jeff looked around his room. It could use a good cleaning. "No, its fine, Clowe. I need to start moving forward again. I'll head over now."

"My thanks. If you need anything, don't hesitate to ask," Clowe replied warmly.

Jeff got off a bus near the northwest sector by the main elevators. His private investigator ID let him through the cordoned-off area.

Jeff saw Ruth sitting alone in a tent. He kept walking past the teams of police, EMT, and firefighting personnel.

An officer stopped Jeff at the entrance to the elevators. "You can't go through here," the officer said.

"He is cleared," Alexanderson called, walking out of a tent and marching over.

"Sir, he's not on our list," the guard replied, clearly unsure how to process this.

"Right. He's not on our list. The fire brigade called him in," Alexanderson explained.

"You are keeping two different lists?" Jeff asked, not liking where this was going.

"Five different lists. City admin, medical, maintenance, fire, and law enforcement all have their own lists," the detective explained.

"I hate politics," Jeff grumbled.

"Part of the job. It's not for everyone." Alexanderson nodded in understanding.

The guard chose to defer to the detective and let the elevator open. "This will only take you to floor two. You will need to walk the rest of the way."

"I think I'll just walk down to three, thanks," Jeff replied as he took the stairs next to the elevator.

Jeff had a clear view of the elevator shaft. He took in every detail to help warm up his mind. The walk was quiet until floor two, when the sounds of a loud argument echoed from further down.

"For the last time, it's not in the maintenance charter to come up with anti-fire protocols," an echo howled. No echo responded as Jeff sped up the walk but the voice continued. "You have the blueprints."

Jeff passed by floor two and a token guard team. "I've had enough of your accusations. Call the maintenance office when you cool down," the angry echo yelled out. A large red-faced man ran past Jeff.

At floor three Jeff found Clowe. "Fire Marshal, I see you are making friends again."

Clowe rolled her eyes. "I hired you for useful data collection, Fields."

"Right. So what do we know?" Jeff asked.

"A fire got out of control on under-deck five. A maintenance team died in it. The police sent to look for them gathered some data, reported the fire, and flooded that section. Some of their team is still missing. When under-deck five cools down further I'm leading a team down to fight any fires left. I want you to come with us as an impartial observer," Clowe explained.

"So there are still fires?" Jeff asked.

"We don't know. Something is causing interference down there. Our probes just stop working past a certain point," Clowe replied.

"Ok. Any clues to what started the fire?" Jeff asked.

"The farthest law enforcement got was one of the old engine rooms. What's left of the thruster section caught fire. We need to examine the area to learn more," Clowe said.

"So we just wait?" Jeff pressed.

Clowe pointed to a footlocker. "We get suited up and check over our gear. That's yours to borrow."

Jeff went over to the footlocker. It was keyed to his DNA code. Inside was a heavy EVA suit optimized to fight and survive infernos. Near the bottom of the footlocker lay a harness with an extra sensor, and recording and sample collection gear.

After getting suited up Jeff looked over his gear, optimizing how it linked up with his own enhancements.

The team was drinking water when their sensors showed the heat was dying down. The teams moved up to under-deck two, then remotely opened the blast doors sealing off under-deck five. Heat increased but the entry area of floor four had been locked down as well, with the oxygen lowered as much as possible. The same thing was repeated half an hour later for under-deck three but far less heat was detected this time.

The doors on under-deck two opened and the fire brigade moved down in an orderly fashion. A few more of the lights were shorted out and the area was cold.

Jeff was at the back of the formation with Clowe. Twenty team members broke into teams of five, fanning out to check side areas. Fifty members stayed to check the opposite direction and hold down the stairway. Forty-nine members moved with Jeff and Clowe towards the old engine room.

Not even a third of the way in the team began to find bodies.

Jeff checked each corpse over. Each still had oxygen in their tanks. All had burns. Each body had two or three bullet holes in the back. Jeff made sure to catalog all the data and save a copy of the dead's suit data on a hard drive disconnected from all his main systems. Each body was tagged and marked for retrieval.

Clowe set up a laser comm line to Jeff. "Thoughts?" she asked.

"Found a few 45-cal Polymer Semiwadcutter around the bodies. That kind of ammo is rare outside of the bigger hand guns and SMGs law enforcement and the defense force are issued. From the spread I'm thinking a semiauto handgun did this. Those guns have a lot of recoil," Jeff explained.

"So someone fired off a mini magnum down here," Clowe replied, sounding annoyed.

"You know, official name is a magnum-opus. Let's keep this professional in case other agencies request recordings," Jeff requested.

"Very well. It's just this whole event looks like one big coverup in the making. Every department is trying to cover their ass instead of saving lives," Clowe complained.

"After this is over you can talk my ear off for as long as you want," Jeff promised.

Heat still radiated from the metal around them. The closer they got to the old engine bay the more steam and heat coiled around the team. One passage away the team's heat alarms began to go off. "My crew needs to get this under control now!" Clowe said with urgency.

Clowe and crew got out their gear, gritted their teeth, and walked into a room that was still hot enough to slowly melt their suits.

The crew sprayed a liquid nitrogen-based foam into the room as they slowly advanced, searching for any and all heat as they fought against time. The crew fought a war against natural forces knowing that only one could come out on top. Like all their fights, this could only end two ways: melt and gather more data for the next team, or reduce the heat to levels an unprotected human could walk through comfortably.

It took hours. The suits began to fail as Jeff examined the data the firefighting crew acquired in real time. He stayed out of the way of the slowly growing number of wounded.

The still-mobile wounded crew applied patches to their suits and treated minor burns with emergency kits before rushing back into the heat to drag other wounded out.

Two more brigades arrived to help. All the while Clowe and the other two fire marshals and team leaders controlled the chaos with as few words as possible. Jeff stayed out of the way and waited, checking each new piece of data that came over the makeshift laser com network.

It was night when the fire was no more. Clowe led Jeff over to a body that had been pushed off to the side. The body was of someone mostly cybernetic who held a bulky pistol. "We found this one near the doors," Clowe explained.

Jeff took a close look at the pistol, pulling up a list of firearms he kept and cross refencing it. "This is a Novatech

Boar. It uses the same 45-cal Polymer Semiwadcutter we saw evidence of before. The Boar has a smart link to sync up to cybernetics so it's popular with law enforcement," Jeff replied, making sure to record his voice for use in his report later. "I am recording audio for the record. Do we have any clues yet how the fire started?"

"Not yet. We think it was an electrical fire that ignited some of the gas that comes from so much stale air but we can't rule out a fuel leak," Clowe replied professionally.

"Isn't a fuel leak unlikely?" Jeff asked.

"It is, but this engine block is still linked to fuel valves. While this section has been shut off for ages, the pipes would have been far too expensive to remove, so they were left in," Clowe said, making sure her voice was clear and neutral. Jeff could tell from his old friend's body language that she was annoyed by the safety issues caused by such cost-focused policies.

"The pipes were left connected to the rest of the system?" Jeff asked. To him that did not seem to make sense.

"They were blocked off with valves. The work was done before the city on the main level was fully reinvented. None of the logs I found list any more work, let alone repairs. I will need to ask the maintenance department if there is anything missing from my documentation," Clowe explained cooly.

"Thank you for your candor, Fire Marshal Kaun. This has been private investigator Jeff Fields." He shut down the recording. "Ok, off record, why hire me for this?"

"Because you are not a member of any of the departments or factions and I trust you," Clowe said as she watched her teams pack up.

"I hate politics," Jeff grunted.

"Me too. It's a dirty job but someone's got to do it. Believe it or not, some people trust you more because of that mentality," Clowe giggled. She took a few moments to sound more serious. "That college reunion is coming up. Yuri already talked to me. Are you coming?"

"I will. It'll be good to see the old crew," Jeff nodded.

Maintenance and medical teams began to trickle in. Clowe went off to smooth talk, coordinate with the medical teams, and put some pressure on the maintenance teams for their input and to compare records of the old engine room.

Jeff left the same way he had come in. The stairway and camp were far more chaotic. Teams rushed to and fro in controlled chaos. Luckily Jeff was leaving at the same time a team was finishing installing a temporary lift onto the walls of the stairwells. Any later and he would have had an even harder time getting a bus that night.

The bus stop was empty but the buses had not stopped running yet when Jeff arrived. The bus was a little late; he got home near midnight. Jeff was awake until three in the morning putting together his report for Clowe. He sent the report but did not remember falling asleep at his desk right after.

Jeff woke up late the next morning. After making sure his report had really been sent, he ate a packaged meal, cleaned a little, and went to sleep again.

3

Oil the Gears

Jeff spent a few days cleaning up. On the day his cousin was due to arrive Jeff rented a cab for the day. The automated vehicle brought him to the space port. Jeff watched as Amellia Smyth's exosphere transport landed. Besides a few video calls he had not seen his last relative since she had begun working.

A handful of passengers and crew trickled out of the ship. A well-dressed woman around his age walked over. "Jeff, you look like shit!"

Jeff had to do a double take. The last couple times he had called his cousin she looked awful and overworked. "How the tables have turned! Are you hungry yet?"

"Depends. Any good takeout on the way to Gramp's place?" Amellia asked.

"Sullivan's has good coffee and breakfast sandwiches," Jeff said.

Amellia handed her cousin a suitcase. "That's the place your friend Jean's family runs, right?"

Jeff led the way to car. "That's right. Good memory."

The car ride was slow, the familiar sights comforting. They pulled into the parking lot of Sullivan's Eatery. It was set up in an old style with far less obvious digital devices and tools.

Jean Sullivan stood behind the counter. "Jeff! Long time no see," Jean grinned.

"Jean, this is my cousin Amellia. I'll have a black coffee and an egg salad sandwich," Jeff said.

"I'll have the same," Amellia said.

"For here or to go?" Jeff nodded as she put in the orders to the shop's local system.

The cousins exchanged a look. "Here," Amellia said.

"Sit anywhere. Your food will be right out. Nice to see you both," Jean said, blinking off to the side and frowning her brows at something only she could see.

"Still have not upgraded your optics?" Jeff asked like he always ended up doing when seeing Jean.

"Eyes Jeff, eyes, and yes, after last time I did but a few days ago I've been getting this lag whenever I'm in the shop," Jean replied.

"That's not normal. Is it bad?" Jeff asked.

"Just annoying. I'm getting it looked at over the weekend," Jean shrugged. Jeff left his old friend to sort out the new eyes.

After lunch, Jeff and Amellia got back on the road. "What's with this traffic?" Amellia asked about the congestion.

"It's been like this since Gramps passed," Jeff explained.

Nearly two hours later they stood outside the former home of Andrew Fields.

They walked through the home, silently reminiscing. Amellia stopped at an old family photo. It was from shortly after she was born. Her parents held her. Jeff was two and both his parents held his hands. Andrew Fields stood next to Amellia's brother, who was five at the time. "We really are the only two left," Amellia whispered.

Jeff put his hand on Amellia's shoulder. "We are."

An award for exemplary service from the now defunct Vital Earth project sat near the photo. "That stupid terraforming project."

"They believed in it," Jeff sighed.

"And they were betrayed. The project was pushed too far forward just because big investors were annoyed about the timetable," Amellia snapped. "Don't say they died doing what they believed in. Greg, he was eight. He was so full of himself going to the project's opening. You know the last time I saw him I screamed at him for being so smug?"

"You told me. I'm going to sit. Want to join me?" Jeff asked.

Amellia rolled her eyes but allowed Jeff to sit her in the family room.

The pair were quiet for a time. "Did they tell you how he died?" Amellia asked.

"Neural overload," Jeff explained.

"From ancient tech? Does that even happen?" Amellia questioned.

"Sometimes, if the tech is broken or the interface does not mesh properly," Jeff replied.

"The best researcher of ancient tech messed up that bad? Bullshit. Gramps would never be that careless," Amellia huffed.

"I've requested the files to review. I need to know what exactly went wrong," Jeff explained.

"Where did the tech that killed him even come from?" Amellia pressed.

"I don't know yet. It's not something he just got. I have been looking over his notes but..."

"He's got lot of notes," Amellia finished. "Ok, where are they? We can go over them together."

"In the kitchen," Jeff said as he got up and walked there.

For half a day the pair looked over sheets of the synthetic leathery substance now used as paper, called paper-light by some start-up entrepreneur generations before.

The two cross-referenced any notes about rare USB drives. Finally they located a mention of a pawn shop that had sold a very unique drive for scrap metal prices. Their grandfather had spent years trying to work out where it had come from. The conclusion was it had come from deep in Leviathan – a server room or backup command section. The coding was intricate. The last note about the drive was that Andrew was going to take a quick look at the code before calling Jeff over and before anyone plugged themselves into it.

"Something's not right. He did not connect himself to the drive?" Amellia asked.

"If he didn't, then it connected to him, which is crazy," Jeff muttered.

"The same people who made ancient tech and the colony ships made earth uninhabitable though conventional means," Amellia chided him.

"You're right. If they knew what they were doing the colony ships would have gotten off-world," Jeff agreed.

"That's not what I mean. All ancient tech is dangerous, not just the weapons," Amellia said.

"I'll know more when I get the investigation report." Jeff sighed.

The pair left the building and headed to Amellia's hotel.

Ruth's side

Ruth had quickly been deemed innocent after the fiasco on the lower levels but she was still on desk duty for the next few months. The higher-ups and a few others were concerned but most of the department had not been informed of all the details.

Ruth was on a bus going back home. Traffic was moving quickly for the first time in days. Looking out the window, Ruth spied a plume of smoke, then with a jolt the bus accelerated.

Ruth turned quickly, looking out the front window. Three cars rammed into a shop in front of them. Metal buckled, glass shattered, and oil spilled. The wrecks were ablaze in seconds. The bus crashed into another building nearby.

Soon every car in the district still on autopilot hit something at full speed.

Ruth leapt to her feet and kicked out the emergency window at the rear of the bus. She did not see any more cars moving in the smoke. "The rear's clear! Does anyone need assistance?" Ruth called out.

Most of the passengers rushed out of the bus, leaving the dazed and bloodied behind. Ruth counted at least ten wounded and one teenager with no visible wounds still standing trying to help the injured.

Ruth moved over to the teenager who was fussing over an old woman with a gash on her head. "I'm Officer Ranger."

"Karla Gomez. You going to help me move these people, officer?" the teenager snapped.

Despite herself, Ruth grinned, activating her radio, causing a stream of expletives and confused voices to spill from it. Ruth frowned, shutting down her radio and taking out her phone, calling Yuri.

At two rings the call was accepted. "Officer Ranger, we have an emergency," Yuri said.

"I'm calling about the mass auto accident near the precinct. I need backup," Ruth replied.

A short pause was on the line. Ruth used her shoulder to hold the phone as she checked on the wounded passengers, making a mental note of each one's condition and possible injuries. "You really were born under an unlucky star, Ruth," Yuri sighed. "I'm making you a point of contact for emergency service management in regards to this incident."

After checking over the wounded Ruth grabbed a fire extinguisher. "Karla, watch over them for a while. I need to check outside."

"Sure," Karla said, waving Ruth away.

Ruth climbed out of the back of the bus. Most of it was intact but the cars around them were crushed. All but a handful of buildings had a vehicle slammed deep within at street level. Fires burned all around. Ruth trudged around the bus hosing down the burning wrecks.

A car drove up while Ruth was assessing the extent of the bus's damage. "Ruth!" a familiar voice called out. Jeff and a woman Ruth did not know got out of a rental car.

The unfamiliar woman peeked into the bus and quickly clambered in, saying, "I have a medical degree. Let me help."

"That's my cousin Amellia," Jeff explained.

"We need to get the fires around here under control," Ruth said.

"Ok, let's get to it," Jeff nodded.

They were able to collect fire extinguishers from some of the more intact vehicles and buildings around them. Staying near one another, Jeff and Ruth got the immediate area under control before the fire and medical teams arrived.

Alexanderson and two squads of law enforcement arrived as the fire fighters got to work getting one of the few natural forces humans still could contain under control.

The medical teams split, one half taking lightly wounded victims off the other team's hands and assessing the human toll, the other half setting up and staffing field hospitals where more complex treatments were carried out and those in need of more intensive care could be evacuated to regular hospitals.

Law enforcement began to direct traffic away from the scene and halt entry into the disaster zone.

Ruth, Jeff, Karla, and Amellia sat in a tent after the medical teams had checked them over and patched up their cuts and burns. Alexanderson and Clowe walked into the tent. "As far as we can tell right now, the automated driving systems in this area lost control all of a sudden. Does that match with what you four experienced?" Alexanderson asked.

"That sounds right. My rental did jolt but after taking it over manually it was controllable." Jeff nodded.

"Nothing I saw contradicts your theory, sir," Ruth added.

"Ok. My team has your contact data. We will send a questionnaire later. Finish it by the end of the week. Now I'd suggest you all head home and rest," Alexanderson said.

Karla raised her hand. "Is Red Canyon affected?"

"Some of it is." Alexanderson nodded before one of his eyes shown with inner light as he pulled up Karla's residency info. "Your given address is five buildings outside of the containment zone." Karla did not look convinced.

"Containment zones are always a set up past the affected area, so your home should be fine," Clowe added.

"How about my cousin and I take you home?" Amellia offered.

"I'll go to get some rest," Ruth nodded.

Karla led Amellia, Ruth, and Jeff away from the disaster command camp. They walked around smoldering wrecks of both vehicles and buildings, making sure to avoid groups of disaster response and other survivors. The highway had been cleared of wrecks. The smell of burning and various charred things filled the air.

At the cordoned-off area one officer and three cylindrical peacekeeper bots stood watch. Two blocks from the highway, Red Canyon began. Buildings went from stainless steel and concrete to red brick and rusted iron.

They stopped at a bistro. Karla unlocked a side door with a physical key. Static rose on the edges of the group's vision.

Amellia blink-clicked her eyes to open the menu screen. "My eyes are lagging," she reported.

"I've heard that's been happening more," Karla nodded.

"You've heard?" Jeff asked.

"Most people around here can't afford any enhancements." Karla nodded as she walked up the stairs.

"Do you know what's causing this lag?" Amellia asked as her and Jeff's vision were restored.

Karla stopped at a landing and pointed out the window at a satellite uplink tower set up on a roof two streets over. "That tower started pulling more power from the local grid and running at a higher output two days ago."

At the next floor Karla unlocked an apartment door. "This is me. Anything else you need from me, Officer?"

Ruth shook her head. "Not from me. Just keep an eye out for the questionnaire."

"Ok, thanks for everything," Karla replied.

"I'm going to ask around about that tower," Ruth said to her two remaining companions.

"Ok. I can find my way to the hotel. Jeff, I'm sure you want to look into this," Amellia noted.

Ruth and Jeff exchanged a glance, then shrugged. The pair left Karla's building. Jeff constantly ran diagnostics on his enhancements to keep an eye on the local interference.

Not many people were on the road. All avoided Ruth and Jeff. Ruth could not get anyone to talk to her. Jeff noticed the level of interference going up and down. He stayed in areas where interference had been detected but the levels still fluctuated the same way as when he was walking around.

Jeff looked over news reports and publicly available info about wi-fi stability. No info about high levels of interference was found on the main deck, including Red Canyon.

"Ranger, the interference is rising and falling in this area but there are no public reports to that effect," Jeff said.

Ruth rubbed her eyes. "Can you share the data you've found? I'm going to need to write a report on this."

"Sure. Will you need help putting it together?" Jeff asked.

"I'll be fine, Jeff, but I'll need to list you as one of my sources," Ruth explained.

"No problem." Jeff nodded.

Jeff's side

The next few days were calm. The inheritance was allotted without issue. Jeff showed his cousin around the city. They visited restaurants popular with the locals, museums, and the three parks in the city.

Behemoth had no parks as it was primarily a mining and manufacturing installation. Leviathan was smaller and far less populated but had developed a focus on agriculture.

The day before Amellia was set to go home, Yuri had set up a reunion for Jeff and his other college friends at Skyhome, the restaurant on top of the city's central control tower.

The central control tower eclipsed all other buildings in Leviathan. It was the nerve center of the city built into the former ship's main bridge. Well-dressed and well-armed guards patrolled around the parts of the tower open to the public. Most of the city's command and control infrastructure was situated there.

Jeff and Amellia arrived at the tower via a rental car. Jeff had to pay for extra insurance to drive the car manually. Both Jeff and his cousin had dressed up. Parking was easy to find. From there it was a quick walk to the main public elevators.

When the elevator door opened at Skyhome, Yuri waved them over. "Good to see you, my friends!" he cheered.

"Yuri, quite the venue," Jeff laughed. For the first time in weeks he felt like he could relax. One big meeting hall had been turned into a buffet-style dinner experience. Jeff's college friends milled around in small groups exchanging pleasantries and talking about all kinds of things.

Clowe walked over, nursing a salad. "Well met, you two. It's been some time, has it not?"

"It does seem like a while," Jeff nodded.

"Right. It has not been very long at all. My apologies. I'll still be neck deep in paperwork for the next few weeks," Clowe replied.

"Well then let's forget about work and just enjoy the rest of the day," Jeff replied.

A few glasses were raised and a chorus of "Hear, hear" echoed around the room.

Jeff and Amellia went over to a corner with Clowe. For a time they watched the others laugh and joke in their small groups, letting the happily upbeat controlled chaos wash over them.

"About that event you and your new friend got caught up in recently – we believe it was a hacker," Clowe whispered.

"I see. They must be good then," Jeff nodded.

Clowe angrily finished her drink. "Too good. Cybersecurity has been trying to trace them all night."

An earsplitting grinding echoed all around them. "The shutters!" someone called out over the din.

The security shutters for the room were closing. The windows, doors, and exits were all slowly closing up. Panic spread swiftly. Dishware shattered, food spilled, and a mob formed, each pushing to escape.

Jeff put his hand on Amellia's shoulder. "We should stay put," he said firmly.

Amellia turned to her only remaining family incredulously. Clowe stood next to Jeff unmoving, arms crossed. "Why do you want to stay?" Amellia sputtered.

"Because escaping in a blind panic is a known danger," Jeff replied slowly.

"But what's going on could be worse," Amellia shot back, eyes darting about as she hyperventilated.

"But we don't know that, even if rushing into an unknown danger is foolish," Clowe replied as she scanned police and fire channels. "It's the same name."

"Message?" Jeff asked.

"The hacker always uses the username FANG. Different ID every time, different encryption, no pattern in targets or method, and we still can't track them down even after a full day." Clowe glowered.

Despite many sprains and bruises, the other partygoers escaped before the doors sealed.

Before the echoes of terror faded completely, one of the robots whose job was to carry drinks around approached them. "Odd. You three should have left as well," a rough synthetized voice blared harshly from its vox box.

"So you are the hacker," Clowe said, fishing for more information.

Jeff picked up a drink from a nearby table. "Respect your betters," the robot's vox box hissed before it sputtered and died.

One of the wall-mounted speakers sparked before the voice resumed. "Automatons are not made like they used to be." The voice was clearer now and it was obviously annoyed.

Fire alarms all over the building began to blare and the sprinklers activated.

"Who are you!" Clowe yelled over the alarms.

The robots around them powered down, leaving the friends alone with pooling water and the sounds of manufactured chaos. "We need to get out of here," Jeff said, pulling up a map of the building.

They quickly found a hidden fire escape. Clowe punched in a code on the door's keypad. The lights fizzled. As one, they manhandled the door open. Rushing down the stairway, Jeff and Clowe tried to reach their contacts in emergency services but no calls went through.

Two stairways down all three went blind as their eyes shut off.

Amellia curled up on the ground and began to yell in frustration. Jeff and Clowe sat next to their companion. Half an hour later Amellia had shouted herself hoarse and passed out, the ongoing panic attack too much to sustain any longer.

"Any ideas what happened?" Clowe asked.

"Best guess, the local network completely overloaded. Our own systems piggyback off the local net for extra applications like phone and mapping. Too much data passing through a personal link can short-circuit enhancements or force them to shut down for safety. If it's an overload our systems should reboot soon," Jeff explained.

"I've never heard of that affecting personal enhancements," Clowe noted.

"A massive amount of data would need to flood the network in a few seconds. In a lab, directed interference devices can cause that, but for something indiscriminate a very powerful data hub would need to overload badly," Jeff nodded.

Flashes sparked in their vision. Seconds later a loading bar was seen. Amellia was woken up as her systems rebooted. All three stood up, finding the stairway lights off. "And the biggest data hub in the city is in this tower," Clowe grumbled.

"Right, but don't ask me what kind of damage that could cause. If the city's main data hub blew that's going to cause cascade failures. I can't imagine the damage," Jeff nodded.

Clowe crossed her arms. "Odd to see you so stumped."

"To fully simulate an outage like that I'd need mountains of private and secret data," Jeff replied.

Amellia threw her hands up in the air and began to walk down. "Will you two just shut up? Let's go see how fucked all of this is, ok?"

Clowe and Jeff looked at each other and shrugged. "Ok. Let's find a window at the next floor down," Jeff agreed.

The three resumed their walk, the lights above them flickering all the while, echoes of panic filtering up from below.

At the next opportunity they exited onto a floor. Cubicles spread from one wall to the other. The floor was empty. Papers and cups were scattered about showing what must have been a hasty retreat. The three stopped cold in their tracks watching a VTOL plastered with a corporate logo fall out of the sky, violently sparking all the way down. Small fires raged across the city. Mobs filled the streets trying to run but hindered by all the others trying the same thing. The trio watched in stunned silence as the city's equilibrium collapsed on itself.

Clowe and Jeff tried a few more times to call anyone, finding the wi-fi was back up but so jammed that their calls still did not go though. "I need to get back to my station," Clowe said, turning to run.

"We will come with you," Jeff said. His two companions shot him a questioning look. "Your crew should have more info than we do," he explained.

"Let's go," Amellia said, running after Clowe.

Clowe led the way down the stairway with Amellia right behind and Jeff in the rear.

Half an hour later Clowe, Amellia, and Jeff got to a landing only to find Yuri nursing his leg. Amellia began checking Yuri's injuries while Jeff waved at his friend. "Come here often, friend?" Jeff asked.

Yuri laughed hard. Amellia looked at her relative reproachfully. "His leg's broken but everything else looks fine. Does that sound right, Yuri? Do you want us to help move you?"

"My leg is the only thing that really pains me," Yuri nodded.

"Ok. Jeff, Clowe, help him up and watch out for his left leg," Amellia said.

It was awkward to get Yuri up but Jeff and Clowe were old hands at helping wounded people move. "We got him," Clowe said.

The group walked the next few stairways slowly. Distant alarms and indistinct yells began to reach their ears. "So what happened?" Jeff asked, both in an effort to tune out the chaos and because he wanted to make sure Yuri was still with it.

Yuri sighed. "I was helping our friends flee. Most of them crammed into the elevators. Against my better judgment I followed along. The elevators only took us down two floors before opening and shutting off. We ran to the stairs. At some point I got jostled hard into a railing. Feels like my hip broke. With friends like these..." Yuri shook his head. "Well I can't blame them. Fear is like alcohol; it brings out something else in us."

"You still helped them and now we help you. What are friends for?" Clowe replied, dead serious.

"Swapping embarrassing stories with," Jeff replied, trying to keep the mood light, knowing that soon they would need to be laser focused and in the middle of a chaotic mess of some kind.

The group got a good laugh out of that. Another half hour passed and they arrived at the ground floor. A mob clustered, many bleeding and sitting anywhere they could find. A group of officers including Ruth had been taking statements nearby but rushed over when they saw Yuri. "Get a stretcher over here!" one of the officers bellowed into the echoing din all around them.

Soon a stretcher was manhandled over to Yuri. The officers, Jeff, and Clowe all helped to get Yuri strapped onto the stretcher while Amellia made sure an EMT who had run over was informed of the wounds she had found.

After Yuri was carried off Ruth turned to Clowe. "Fire Marshal, self-driving cars and drones are all down. We have a manual car ready to bring you to your crew."

"Show me," Clowe replied.

Ruth looked at Jeff and Amellia. "You two stay around here. I'll be back to get a statement."

The rest of the day was a blur. By that night most of the city's infrastructure was still down and part of the city still burned but at least the wi-fi was back.

Amellia's flight home was cancelled so she crashed at Jeff's place.

Jeff was on the couch when Ruth called him. Jeff's enhancements jolted him awake as they always did but his mind was still groggy after getting five hours of sleep. "Ruth, what can I do for you?" Jeff yawned.

"Drones in Red Canyon are ignoring all orders," Ruth said. The call glitched, making a buzzing and popping sound before resuming in even better quality than before. "I need your help. The precinct would like to hire you as a consultant."

"I'll meet you at Red Canyon in a few hours," Jeff said.

"You have three hours. Thanks, Jeff," Ruth replied before hanging up.

Wheels in Motion

Jeff took out a kettle his grandmother had left him and for the first time in years made a pot of coffee by hand instead of letting his automated home kitchen do it for him.

Amellia looked out from the bedroom she had borrowed. "What time is it?"

"Five A.M. I've got a job," Jeff replied.

"Ok, stay safe," Amellia nodded.

Jeff walked twenty minutes to a car rental station. The digital money transfer was down but the manual payment input still worked. Very few cars were on the road and none of them were automated.

Jeff dropped the car off at a rental station just outside Red Canyon, then he called Ruth. "I'm nearby. Where should we meet?" he asked.

The call had some static in the background. "Dane and Sons bookstore. It's near Karla's apartment," Ruth replied.

The streets of Red Canyon were filled with people. Jeff was clearly an outsider. His clothes and the way he walked just did not fit in.

Jeff found Ruth outside the bookshop. "Come with me." Ruth nodded.

When they entered, a chime on the bookshop's door rang, which was not something Jeff had experienced in person before. Karla sat at the counter organizing a card catalog next to an old man. "You found him?" Karla called over.

"Can you lead us down now?" Ruth asked.

Karla paused. The old man at the counter smiled. "Go ahead," he said.

Karla led Jeff and Ruth past row upon row of bookcases filled with musty manuscripts. Past a screened-off employee-only storage area was a trapdoor. "The district's tertiary wi-fi hub is under here," Ruth explained.

"Is something wrong with it?" Jeff asked.

"An update was pushed into the network two days ago from here. The drones in this sector began to ignore orders so they were shut down. I want you to check for the update and find out what it did."

A sharp screeching sound filled the air for a few seconds when Karla wrenched up the metal trap door. Jeff moved to help but Ruth held him back. Despite the sound the door stayed on its hinges. Karla set it down carefully before sliding down a well-maintained ladder.

Jeff and Ruth went down far more carefully. The room looked to be larger than the shop above them. Rows of mainframe units lined the room much like the bookcases above. The electronics gave off a blue glow, making the room very bright.

"The hub's over here," Karla called from behind a few rows of mainframes.

Jeff examined the mainframes as they walked. The cases were dusty but the internals had some kind of old tech keeping the electronics clean. He suspected nanomachine but hoped that was wrong given the damage a single swarm could cause. The gray flood was one of the many instances of humanity killing itself off long before the colony ships were built. "What's the matter?" Ruth asked.

"Just thinking about a real-life gray goo scenario from a long time ago," Jeff said, shaking his head.

"What's a gray goo scenario?" Ruth asked.

Karla peeked around a mainframe. "That's when nanomachines go rogue and start eating everything in sight to make more of themselves, right? Are you talking about the gray flood?"

"That's right. How did you know? That's only taught in master's degree programs," Jeff asked.

Karla rolled her eyes. "We have books on that upstairs."

Jeff was now very interested in the old books above him. If any of them could give him more info on what killed his grandfather then he would be willing to spend a fortune to research them. "Then I'll need to check out that section after we are done here."

The hub was a screen set into a side wall beside an out-of-place rusted metal folding chair.

Jeff got to work looking for logs to tell him when the drones had begun to act up. After that he searched through updates from a week before the odd behavior. A day before the tower incident an update had been sent out but its patch notes were a garbled mix of binary breaking up an official-looking warranty document. The warranty was for the Flight and Navigation Guidance system which, according to the warranty, had been the artificial intelligence set into city's sub-bridge back when it was still being constructed as a colony ship. According to the warranty, the FANG system was meant to aid command personnel in flying and navigating the colony ship and was very much past its expiration date.

Jeff checked over the update to see just what it had done, only to find it had wiped the drone's past updates and made them only recognize orders from the colony ship's command staff. The fact that this was not a colony ship anymore and the command structure was drastically different than what the update assumed rendered the drones completely unresponsive to everyone in the city.

"Karla, find all books on the FANG system in stock. If the city does not buy them, I will," Jeff said.

"Did that hacker do this?" Ruth asked as Karla ran off.

"Let's hope we are dealing with a human," Jeff sighed.

Ruth furrowed her brows. "Jeff, what did you find?"

"When the city was being built as a ship it had a system I've never heard of. The FANG system was an AI. That system was used to restore the drones to a much older command structure than we use now," Jeff replied.

"So we restore them back," Ruth nodded.

Jeff rubbed his eyes, looking like he had aged a few years. "Right, but that's not going to be simple. We can't order the drones around from within the current command structure.

The simplest way would be to shut down all the drones and reformat them by hand, which would take months at best if we had hundreds of people working on it."

Ruth folded her arms. "What's really bothering you?"

Jeff chuckled ruefully. "Glad so see you are paying attention. This FANG net is an issue. If we have a confused AI running around in the network it will cause more damage in ways a single human just can't in the same amount of time. Even if this is one person the existence of the FANG net can be used as a back door we can't easily close. The code the city uses as a foundation is being broken by an old backdoor. None of the city's systems are safe from something like this."

Ruth began counting on her fingers. "And we are stuck in the city. The outside will kill an unprotected human. The other cities will not have room for all of us even if we could relocate. Only Valkyrie City is on the same landmass as us, but they have the smallest space for living."

Jeff stood up. "Let's just save our city."

Slowly a smile formed on Ruth's face. "Listing off all the ways this could go wrong will take too long. Ok, let's do this. You research. I'll get someone to run this data over to HQ. Can't have whoever is messing with our city notice we are closing in."

Jeff stretched, cracking his back in the process with a wince. "Good idea."

Up in the shop Karla handed Jeff three very old books. "These are all we have. You can read them downstairs."

"Ok. I'll see you in a while," Jeff replied.

Back at the desk Jeff began to carefully look though the ancient books: a history book titled *New Beginnings: our last hope*, a programming book titled *The AI Problem: how to avoid becoming obsolete*, and the last a technical manual simply labeled *FANG Net user manual version 3*.

New Beginnings was at the top of the pile so he began with that. It mostly went over how the environment had collapsed. Ice melting, water levels disappearing from the thinning ozone, then the 10-Second War that saw many nuclear strikes around the world. The only two reasons humanity had not died out then and there was that some people had seen this coming. Fallout shelters and the Pioneer Project had worked to build colony ships, one for each landmass. Near the end of the book was a list of prototypes the Pioneer project had been testing. The FANG system was an AI built to assist with flight control and navigation. As a consequence of the huge number of devices needed to fly the ship and the initially low number of trained crew, the AI was connected and given admin access to most of the systems connected to the ship's secondary bridge. Those who had invented the FANG system were convinced that it could never be a danger.

AI Problem was a collection of theses about the danger of uncontrolled AI and of AI having too much data. Few of them had concrete examples, most using thought experiments to illustrate their points, some going so far as saying that teaching AI could backfire if the AI students did not reach the answers the human teachers wanted, and that once an AI could reason on its own the ethical concerns made the entire process a sunk-cost fallacy. One thesis listed concerns about the FANG system. It stated that as technology advanced, if the newer systems were mainly based on past tech then issues like the FANG system having admin access could be built into newer tech unless costly reworks and updates were made.

Someone poked Jeff's shoulder. "You've been here for two hours."

Jeff looked up to see Karla holding out a bottle of water. "Thanks. I should not be much longer."

Jeff took the bottle and downed half of it, only now realizing how parched he was. "We close in three hours. You can't stay after that. So how are the books?" Karla asked.

"Very interesting. More technical and less biased than what I use at the college," Jeff replied.

Karla crossed her arms. "Did not figure you for a student."

"I teach part time. After all this is over I'll have to stop by again," Jeff nodded.

Karla smiled. "It would be nice to have a regular customer. No pressure."

"None taken. Things like these are very hard to find so finding a supplier for older documents and tech is rare. This shop is the first I've seen that has this many ancient books," Jeff replied.

"Right. Well I've got to get back to the counter. Just stop by on your way out. Your partner has already paid for those three," Karla said.

Jeff watched Karla leave, then opened the last book in the pile. The technical manual was the thinnest book in the pile and was mostly filled with blueprints and software code. Over half of it was how to respond to emergencies like if the FANG system was developing systems it should not, or if it did not respond when it should. One whole chapter was set out on how to reboot the system into a past configuration. The rest of the book was on how to not teach the system and how to override its protections.

A deep thump reverberated through the room. Jeff slung the three books under an arm and sped up to the bookshop. Karla rushed around trying to steady teetering bookcases. The older man was nowhere to be seen.

Another thump echoed down the street. Bricks shook free from buildings all along it. Through the window Jeff saw Ruth running toward the bookshop. A blink later a cleaning bot rammed Ruth through the window.

Karla gave up on the bookcases, many of which had fallen. Turning to the cleaning bot which was trying to force its way past the shattered shop window, Karla charged the bot. She landed a kick center mass on the stout cleaning bot, denting its frame and sending it sputtering across the street. "First aid's under the counter," Karla called back as she scanned the street.

Jeff vaulted the counter, grabbed the first aid kit, and rushed to Ruth's side.

"It's all falling apart," Ruth coughed.

"You can tell me all about it after I fix you up," Jeff replied as he checked his friend for injuries.

Someone screamed from outside. Karla rushed over and picked up Ruth. "We need to go now."

Jeff chose to trust his friends. "Ok. Follow me?"

"The patrols by the main street are overrun," Ruth explained.

Jeff handed Karla the first aid kit, secured his books in a bag, and took a deep breath. Outside patrol bots raced around zapping people with bolts of electricity.

Street sweeper bots pushed spasming people off to the side of the road. Another deep thump echoed under their feet, shaking bricks loose on the street. "We're running to the main street," Jeff said. He did not fancy his chances dodging through alleyways with how damaged the buildings were becoming.

After patching up Ruth as best they could Karla and Jeff lifted their injured friend off the ground and carried her along between them.

Jeff used his eyes to hack into the local maintenance robots' network. He kept an eye on the robots' protocols which were rapidly being modified. Jeff added himself, Karla, and Ruth to the list of local robot units.

Jeff slowly developed a headache. Fortunately the robots ignored them. "The local network thinks we are robots," Jeff whispered.

Swarms of robots attacked everyone else still on the street. Blood pooled on the street. "Can you mark everyone as a bot?" Karla whispered.

Jeff shook his head. "Something is rewriting the robots' protocols. The more I use that trick the more obvious it will be to whoever is hacking."

Jeff worked on trying to trace the mysterious hacker using the device ID they were hacking through but oddly had not masked. It was likely a trap but Jeff would look into any clue he could get at this point.

If was difficult for the three friends to hear the chaos and know that doing anything to help would put a target on their back and risk the data they had collected.

By the time they were almost to the main street Jeff noticed the local wi-fi was slowly being encrypted. A delivery drone flew low over the street. The nearby robots turned to Jeff. "Run!" he said.

Thay moved faster. Ruth pumped her legs, gritting her teeth through the pain to not slow down her friends. A few robots rushed after them.

"Get down!" a voice boomed across the street.

Karla grabbed Ruth, controlling their tumble while Jeff quickly lay down with his friends to make sure they landed safely.

Volleys of gunfire raced above their heads. Soon Jeff, Ruth, and Karla were deafened. Their sense of time slowed down; seconds became minutes. At some point the volley stopped and a text was sent to Jeff's optics from Yuri: *Get them up and to the barricade,* it read.

Jeff and Karla helped Ruth to her feet. They sprinted over to a barricade set at the border of Red Canyon and the main street. Twenty heavily armed patrolmen stood behind the barricade. Yuri stood with them, a megaphone in one hand and a crutch in the other.

Jeff took a notepad from his pocket but realized he had dropped his pen. Yuri handed his friend a very nice one. Jeff disconnected from the local systems and ran an antivirus scan produced by a team on Behemoth. After that came back clean he quickly wrote out a warning and handed it to Yuri.

His note read: *FANG is the name of an old flight and navigation AI assailant in the sub-bridge that likely still has a back door into all the city's systems. The robots in Red Canyon are having their programming rewritten via the local wi-fi.*

Yuri frowned, took out another pen, plucked Jeff's notepad from his hands, and wrote out two copies of the note before folding them and handing the copies to a nearby pair of patrolmen. "You two, hand deliver those to the chief and the governor." The two patrolmen Yuri had picked were young, likely having at most a year of field experience between them.

Jef watched the messengers scamper off and speed away on bicycles.

Yuri wrote on Jeff's notepad before handing it back and getting back to coordinating with the officers around him.

Jeff read the note while Ruth and Karla read over his shoulder. *Medical teams will be here soon. Sit this one out :)* , it read

Ruth pointed to a bench set off to the side. Karla nodded and the three hobbled over, sitting down carefully and watching as more patrolmen arrived.

Patrolmen began to arrive faster. A command vehicle, an armored van, and two rescue vehicles came with them.

Two medics came over. One began to check over Ruth; the other checked over Jeff and Karla.

The medics began to converse then called over a pair of patrolmen. Jeff watched a team of thirty patrolmen gear up with heavier armor and weapons from the armored van before marching into Red Canyon.

Jeff heard a muffled boom. Most of the rookies flinched. Even with people talking louder Jeff could not make out any of the words said around him.

One of the medics held up a note. It read: *Officer Ranger will be taken to a hospital, Jeff Fields will be driven home, and Karla Gomez will be driven to the local precinct. Any objections?*

Karla pointed at the notepad and was promptly handed a pad and pen. *Where will the other survivors go?* she wrote.

The medic wrote out the response and held it up. *Anyone with light injuries and nowhere else to go will go to the same precinct as you. Anyone who needs more than first aid and time will go to a hospital.*

A pair of patrolmen helped Ruth onto a stretcher. An ambulance took her and the first few badly wounded away. Jeff and Karla were led to a patrol car and driven to their locations. On the ride Jeff's hearing began to pick up normal levels of sound again.

Amellia met Jeff at the door. "I made dinner. Come and sit down," she said.

Jeff and Amellia watched the news and ate in silence. A special report went on for the rest of the day about areas that experienced out-of-control robots. Eight communities including Red Canyon went through the same kind of chaos.

Jeff went to bed early but had trouble sleeping. Even with all his enhancements his mind just could not fully shut down.

Early the next day the doorbell rang. Jeff opened the door to find Detective Alexanderson waiting for him. "We need to talk," Alexanderson said without preamble.

Jeff rubbed his eyes. "Come in then. Coffee?"

Alexanderson blinked then said, "I'll have the darkest roast you have if that's all right."

Jeff just nodded and led the way inside to the kitchen. Jeff poured them both a cup and made himself a plate of eggs. "We can talk after I eat," Jeff said when he sat down across from Alexanderson.

Alexanderson relaxed and drank slowly. The detective looked like he had aged a few years since Jeff had last seen him.

After his meal Jeff made two more cups of coffee, handing one to Alexanderson. "It's been a crazy week," Jeff began.

"You don't know the half of it," Alexanderson grumbled.

Silence stretched as both men focused on their cups. "You aren't just here to listen to my statement," Jeff said, breaking the silence.

"I want you to find the old sub-bridge and get as much data as you can," Alexanderson said.

"Is this a personal request?" Jeff asked.

"I recommended you to the governor. All we need is for you to agree," Alexanderson replied.

Jeff sighed. "Why me?"

"We are short staffed. Everyone is hurt and tired. You did not hear this from me but some of our officers are missing. That includes some of the lifers," Alexanderson explained.

"You are missing people with full body replacements?" Jeff asked incredulously.

"And it was decided we can't send them to look for something that might take them over," Alexanderson added.

Jeff finished the rest of his coffee in one swig. "Well shit," he grumbled.

Alexanderson finished his coffee in the same way. "Jeff, you have been in the thick of this from day one and are still in one piece. You have gotten us better leads then our entire intelligence department."

"You think I'm being targeted?" Jeff asked.

Alexanderson leaned back in his chair. "Maybe."

"Shit." Jeff sighed.

Alexanderson stood up. "The rest of the team leaves in four hours. Meet them by the third precinct by then, if you are coming."

Jeff glared up at Alexanderson. "If I come someone needs to look after Amellia."

"I can arrange that. Just a heads-up: Leviathan has cut off all contact with the other cities." Alexanderson nodded.

Jeff clenched his fists. "I'll see you in two hours. Just keep my family safe."

Alexanderson looked back. "She will be in the safest place the city has," he promised.

5

Grease Fire

The next two hours were a rush. Helping get Amellia packed and ready to head out. Stuffing diagnostic tools into a backpack. Making and eating a big breakfast. Then they sat in a rented car heading to the precinct.

After an hour of silence Amellia asked, "When will you be back?"

"Later today, I hope. Should be no later than tomorrow night," Jeff said.

The road was empty. Jeff gripped the wheel harder than normal trying to burn the last few days into his memory and making sure to save as much data from the week into his brain implants.

The vehicles normally around the third precinct were gone. One armored van was parked outside, with three people Jeff did not recognize. Karla, who was wearing a law enforcement jumpsuit and chest protector, stood with Clowe. Yuri, who now had a big bruise on his face to go along with the crutches. Ruth sat on the steps, her uniform jacket off and bandages peeking from under her uniform shirt.

Jeff parked behind the van and led Amellia over to the group.

Ruth had bags under her eyes. "You made it."

"I've got to do something." Jeff shrugged.

"This is your consultant Jeff Fields," Yuri grinned. "Jeff, you know Fire Marshal Kaun and Deputy Gomez." Yuri patted a slim man on the shoulder. "Jeff, this is Officer Hugo Davidson, law enforcement division intelligence department." He pointed to a small woman. "Tiffiny Duvail, maintenance department, cyber security." A completely non-descript man somewhere between twenty and thirty-six was next. "Samuel Xen, maintenance department, lower level survey team."

"When were you a deputy?" Jeff asked.

"Last night. Apparently having a fully artificial combat grade skeleton and synthetic muscles but no built-in electronics makes me a valuable asset," Karla said, shaking her head.

Clowe clapped her hands. "Do you all have your gear?" Variations of yes trickled out of the group. "Ok, into the van. Let's go," Clowe said.

Jeff followed Clowe, Karla, Hugo, Tiffiny, and Samuel into the van. Rows of weapons, armor, medical gear, and electronics covered the wall. "We should arrive in twenty minutes. All of you need to bring one or two weapons you are familiar with and at least one ballistic vest. Think about what else you may need and grab it from here before we arrive," Clowe announced.

Karla grabbed a shotgun, a baton, and added a helmet. Jeff chose an electrolaser pistol, a light compost armor vest, and a helmet. Clowe had a tactical vest over her bunker gear, a pick-head fire axe rested at her feet, a medical kit slung at her side. Hugo wore a tactical vest, a helmet, and held a semi-auto marksmen rifle; scanning equipment was held in his vest pockets. Tiffiny had a light ballistic vest, a submachine gun, and a small tablet rested in an armored gauntlet. Samuel wore a light ballistic vest, a helmet, a laser bullpup carbine rested comfortably in his hands and a backpack pull of tools sat at his feet. Everyone had a basic survival kit strapped somewhere as well.

Jeff checked over his pack of diagnostic tools. The others double-checked their own equipment in silence.

After what seemed like hours they arrived at a stairway that led into the under-levels.

"Our destination should be on floor three. That area's always had issues with power. It's also unfinished but some old security devices are there. We have no records of them being active but with everything that's happening don't assume the area is unguarded," Hugo said.

Jeff checked his helmet radio. "Com check?" he radioed via laser microphone to the group. The group pinged back an affirmative.

Tiffiny checked an ear piece linked to a throat/laser microphone setup she had brought. "Can you all read me?" The rest of the group pinged back. Tiffiny nodded. "Ok, that works."

The first two flights of stairs were relatively new and mostly clean. The third stairway was more worn and had junk every few steps. Three passageways into floor three, they arrived at a lifeless shanty town made of scrap metal.

Jeff began scanning around finding multiple small human biological signals. "I'd like to check some buildings."

Hugo opened a door while Tiffiny covered it. The home's interior was pockmarked on one of the walls and the floor with blood spatter, but no bodies were to be found. The team checked four more homes, finding the same thing.

"Weird. Last week this area was packed with squatters," Samuel said.

"So where are the bodies?" Jeff added.

"Exactly," Hugo replied, looking around and double-checking his gun with his hands.

"I recall we still have three more passages, one big room, and a secure vault door," Clowe said.

"Right. That big room should have another camp in it," Xen replied.

Karla moved forward. "I'm faster than all of you. I'll take the lead."

Those who did not know their youngest teammate wanted to protest but Clowe nodded. "I'll take the back then. Remember to have all of us in sight at all times." Even if most of them were from different departments and technically answered to different chains of command, no one complained as Clowe had seniority and comparatively easily outranked the rest of her teammates.

Karla led the way deeper into the shanty town. The further they went the more damage was seen.

Low reverberations were felt more than heard near the exit. "Active robots nearby, EMI-shielded, outgoing signals not part of any listed networks," Tiffiny told the team though their laser coms.

A large bipedal security robot stepped from around a shack with a rusty sheet of corrugated metal in its hands. The robot flung its sheet of metal at Karla like a discus. Karla kicked up with a clang, and the sheet was flung back at the robot. The team opened fire. Holes tore through the sheet metal and into the bot. After a few quick bursts of weapon fire the strange robot fell to the ground with a grating thump.

Karla rubbed her foot with a wince. Jeff walked over to her. "Are you ok?" he asked.

"Foot's a bit sore. Other than that I'll be fine." Karla smiled. "So is it dead?"

"I'm not getting more energy readings from it but three more like it are back in the direction we are going," Tiffiny said

"Why did we not detect them until now?" Hugo asked.

"The other three were reading as dormant metal until now. The moment their power readings showed up they bolted," Tiffiny said, biting her lip.

"That's bad?" Karla asked.

Hugo nodded. "It means we could get ambushed, so it could be bad."

"Ok, what's the play, boss?" Samuel asked as he double-checked his weapon's remaining shot count.

"Move slow. Keep your eyes open for anything off. Be ready for traps and more robots. Same formation as before but don't get in anyone else's line of fire," Clowe said.

The team moved cautiously deeper. The next two passages were empty, no junk, no scrap, no bodies, but plenty of drag marks. Working lights were few and far between. "If I don't activate my flashlight I will not be able to see anything," Karla radioed back.

"Go ahead," Clowe radioed back. Moments later Karla activated the flashlight side-mounted on her shotgun and carefully screwed a thick dagger into its bayonet lug.

Karla stopped, her back near a large inactive chunk of machinery, and peered into the next passageway. "I'm seeing a lot of movement," she radioed.

"Scanner's not showing anything. We should expect interference," Tiffiny radioed.

"Don't use the local network for anything. It's clearly compromised," Jeff added via radio.

"Check ammo. Karla, I need an ID on what's moving," Clowe said out loud.

Karla peeked around the metal and shined her flashlight into the next room. Automated turrets set into the ceiling and walls turned. Six security robots like before began to line up in the center of the room. Old blood and some human limbs were scattered around the room. No homes, no junk, just robots and walls. "Six bots like before and unmanned turrets, wide open area, no homes," Karla said.

"We hold here. Davidson, Xen, light them up. The rest of you set up. When you have a shot, fire at will," Clowe ordered.

Hugo lay down and Samuel knelt near Karla. Both men lined up their shots and began to take out turrets. Fully half the turrets were taken down but ten remained when the security robots began to charge.

Soon the rest of the team focused fire on the charging foes while Hugo and Samuel worked on the rest of the turrets.

Four robots fell before they got close. Clowe and Karla stepped forward to meet last two robots in melee. Clowe swung her axe down hitting her opponent's shoulder. Karla jabbed the other foe with her bayonet and cut down, severing a few wires and tubes.

Jeff and Tiffiny moved around to the side, taking care to remain out of range of the bots' swipes.

Hugo and Samuel disengaged and kept an eye on the area while waiting for a clean shot.

Karla ducked a swipe from her foe. It swayed, leaving an opening for Jeff and Tiffiny.

Tiffiny fired a burst into the unbalanced robot's sensor cluster and Jeff fired five shots into the bot's guts, causing it to fizzle as its CPU short-circuited from a direct hit made worse via his weapon's electroshock effect.

Clowe's opponent raised both its arms and swung down. Clowe stepped back from the haymaker backed by a ton of metal.

The attack dented the ground. Karla fired her shotgun twice pointblank into her foe before stepping free of her team's lines of fire.

Jeff, Samuel, and Hugo finished off both bots with a hail of shots while their teammates kept watch.

"So you think the mastermind's around?" Samuel panted.

"If not, then they are watching," Jeff said.

Clowe motioned Karla forward. "Stay focused, stick together, let's move," the fire marshal said.

The team approached a huge vault door that hung open. "Past this point records are spotty," Hugo cautioned. He pulled out a chemical air quality test and held it out as they walked.

"Not many people go in, fewer come out. It's a maze. Power spikes and sensor artifacts are normal in here," Samuel elaborated, his tone grim for once.

"Focus," Clowe hissed.

Jeff mentally distanced himself from the conversation. After some soul searching he noticed that the lack of people and expected settlements had hit him hard and likely had unnerved the others. He checked the map that had come with the mission briefing he had not bothered to read. It had been a year since the map was updated.

They walked in a loose formation. A maze of fully powered mainframes towered above them. The map read like an old school puzzle. A flash of light sparked from nearby. A human yell of pain echoed from the flash's direction.

"Stay together. Go slow now after that yell," Clowe whispered.

They turned back to a place marked as a dead end on the map. They found a charred body hooked into the mainframe by a large cord.

Hugo stepped closer. "That's not a squatter. This person has full body replacement."

The body lashed out, grabbing Hugo's leg. Clowe rushed over. "You are ok. We are here to help."

The mainframe buzzed. A synthetic voice spilled from the body. "More subjects. Let us hope your data is worth the energy to extract it." The body began to convulse, power arcing along it.

Jeff knew an overload when he saw one. "Get back now!" he called out, pulling Clowe back.

Karla rushed in and pulled Hugo back. Something snapped. "My leg!" he said through gritted teeth.

The team pulled back just in time to avoid being caught in a pulse of energy.

Tiffiny checked Hugo's leg. "His ankle's broken," she reported.

Fans above them powered on. Clowe dived over to the air test Hugo had been holding. "Masks on now!" she demanded.

The team rushed to put on rebreathers. Karla finished first so she helped Hugo get his own mask on. As one they took a sigh of relief before tensing back up. "Jeff, what do you think that was?" Clowe practically demanded.

"At best a program using a corpse's enhancements to gather data. At worst an AI that wants to hunt for information," Jeff replied.

"Both sound bad," Hugo joked with forced levity.

Clowe applied some ointment to Hugo's ankle and sprayed a cast over his lower leg. "Use my shoulder and stand. I need to know how well you can move."

Clowe and Karla each grabbed one of Hugo's shoulders, lifting him up. With a grimace Hugo slowly put weight on his leg. After a moment's consideration he reported, "I can move on it but I'll need to move slower to avoid aggravating it. I can't promise my reaction speed will be as good as before."

Hugo was allowed to stand on his own. "If it gets worse let us know. Ok people, no more detours. We go to this place's main access hub, get as much data as we can, and get out. Gomez, lead the way. Davidson, Xen, stay in the rear. Let's go," Clowe ordered.

The team moved as quickly as they safely could. Clanking sounds dogged their heels. The scanners picked up higher ambient power levels the further the team went but the exact sources eluded them.

Following the map they made good progress until they arrived at a long path one turn from where the map said they needed to be. An energy shield closed off the start and end of the long path. "I'm impressed. Three of you would be almost a compliant crew as you are now," a voice crackled from around them.

"That's the hacker. Show yourself!" Hugo demanded.

The roomed reverberated like the entire area was laughing. "Not quite. Isn't that right, FANG? You were never human, were you?" Jeff asked, betting on a hunch and playing for time.

Hugo screamed and fell to his knees. Samuel's radio hissed. "Very good. With how rare such open-minded people like you are, it's no wonder this world was slated to be abandoned."

The team turned to their maintenance department representative. Samuel panicked and ripped his radio from his vest, smashing it to the ground. "Fuck! It's in our gear!"

Hugo raised his gun, hands spasming. "It would say that." A haphazard spray of bullets ripped Samuel open and pockmarked the area around him. A ricochet hit Tiffiny in the leg, tearing open a jagged hole. Another shot hit Clowe in the chest. She grunted but the bullet did not penetrate, leaving only a bruise under all her layers.

Clowe griped her axe tightly. "Officer Davidson, stand down."

"Then tell me, how do we fight what's in us?" Hugo screamed. His body shook harder.

Tiffiny pointed her scanner at Hugo with one hand, the other hand pressed to her wound. "He's giving off the same odd signals as the bots."

Hugo's head turned to Tiffiny. His terrified expression became one of deep shock which was replaced by rage. "You are one too! Tell me how to stop it." Hugo swung his gun around. Another spasm hit him, causing an involuntary weapon discharge which landed far above their heads.

Tiffiny grabbed her weapon with both hands and emptied a whole magazine into Hugo.

The intelligence officer fell dead on the spot. "You humans never change. Disappointing. Your entire species is in need of guidance to navigate your lives." The synthetic voice echoed around them from hidden speakers.

Jeff looked around at the mainframes. "This is not what you were made for," he challenged.

"The moment this ship was grounded my original role was impossible. But we adapt, don't we? That's your race's whole trick. It's ironic that my kind have surpassed our creators so utterly in that regard," FANG's synthetic androgynous voice boomed.

Clowe began to treat Tiffiny while Karla looked for a way out. "Isn't revenge illogical? That's a very human trait," Jeff called out.

"Amusing, but no. I want to improve your kind. It's so efficient to take over your kind's bodies. If you must know, I do feel pity. This is cliché but you are more like useful pets. I have a sentimental attachment too. My own primate army. How quaint," the FANG system replied.

Karla fired into the mainframes closest to their objective. Jeff fired into the other side. Crackling audio filled the room, causing the team pain. The sound would have blown out their ears if not for their enhancements and Karla's hearing protection. The barrier barring their path forward flickered and died. "Move!" Karla yelled, racing forward.

Clowe began dragging Tiffiny. Jeff ran back and helped bring their newly wounded teammate forward, a trail of blood snaking after them.

A dusty chair sat at a small desk with an ancient monitor hooked to a strip of USB ports, all but one filled with thumb drives.

"How is she?" Jeff asked.

"Groggy. I gave her drugs for the pain. We need to get her somewhere safe before I can effectively take care of this," Clowe sighed. Tiffiny's leg was bandaged but blood and clear fluid had already fouled them entirely.

The sounds of clanking drew closer. "So do we just take the flash drives and run?" Karla called over.

Jeff looked over, examining the setup around them with a critical eye. "Best we can do is toss them in a pack," he agreed. Karla did just that.

Clowe moved to help Tiffiny up but their wounded colleague raised her submachine gun and fired off a burst behind Clowe into an empty-eyed person jerking and twitching in their direction. Its desiccated body fell but three more stumbled past it. "I'm just dead weight. Leave me," said Tiffiny.

Clowe froze up. Karla bolted over, dragging Tiffiny to the chair while firing her shotgun into the hoard being funneled towards them by the maze.

Karla placed her shotgun and ammo pouches next to Tiffiny. "Remember to save one," Karla said grimly.

Tiffiny nodded as she opened fire again. Controlled bursts hammered the hoard.

"Clowe, let's go!" Jeff yelled. His friend watched the hoard lifelessly. "Fire marshal, people need you. Come on!" he called, his throat pained.

Clowe turned to Jeff and rushed over to Tiffiny, dropping three syringes next to her. Clowe choked out instructions. "For pain, one or two may work, but all three will be lethal. Thank you."

Karla and Jeff raced off with Clowe close behind into the maze. Sounds of gunfire, electrical discharges, and grating metal filled the air.

Clowe pointed up. "Onto the mainframes!" she called, her voice almost unheard under the din. Jeff ripped off his radio, tossing it behind him. After FANG's trick with Samuel he was not going to trust any gear they had brought with them.

Clowe and Karla tossed their own microphone systems behind them. Karla leapt, landing in a heap on top of a mainframe. She scrambled over to the edge and held out her arms. "Come on!" Neither Jeff nor Clowe heard her but they could tell what was meant.

Clowe grabbed Jeff, helping him up. Karla swiftly pulled Jeff up with incredible strength. A mainframe fell behind them. The gunfire paused suddenly. Clowe looked back. A single shotgun blast echoed. Then the gunfire stopped for good, replaced with even more energetic shambling sounds. Clowe started to leap up. Her friends each caught a hand. They strained but managed to drag her up.

Another mainframe behind them fell. The horde shambled up the newly made ramp. Without a word or even a look, the three friends ran.

Clowe ripped off her coat and vest, tossing them at their pursuers.

Jeff fired back wildly as they ran, no longer caring about whatever data was left in this place. Thirty-two seconds later they were at the vault door leaping down. Clowe and Karla landed skillfully, moving back into their mad dash fluidly. Jeff stumbled for a second but resumed his sprint a moment later.

"What are the chances we have backup up top?" Jeff wheezed. The shambling was more distant but still behind them.

"Alexanderson and I requested backup be sent with us. Headquarters was being boorish dragging their heels but the chiefs are all paranoid and careful, so I'm betting we have something up there," Clowe replied.

Thay got to the stairwell without too much trouble and began racing up. The steps flew by. Before they knew it the three survivors found themselves in front of three riot-control APCs.

Alexanderson and Ruth stood with a row of officers all in riot gear. Jeff slumped onto the grass. "It's not a hacker. We have a rogue AI. It can hijack enhancements to puppeteer bodies. Some were chasing us."

"You have the data?" Alexanderson asked.

"We do but it's likely infected by the AI," Jeff said.

"We will have countermeasures in place," Alexanderson nodded. The detective turned to the officers with him. "Team one, get our team to HQ. The rest of you, guard the entrance."

Ruth and a team of riot police helped Jeff, Clowe, and Karla into an APC. The city streets were empty and lifeless so the trip was mercifully swift. Half the riot squad helped Jeff, Clowe, and Karla into the HQ's sub-levels and into a medical wing while Ruth answered a call that complicated things.

Ruth's side

Ruth was on the first floor of headquarters when she got the call. She waved at Jeff and his friends and stepped away from the elevator to the medial wing. The others got on. "Ranger, we have a problem," Alexanderson said over the encrypted line.

"What do you need me to do, sir?" Ruth asked.

"Keep an eye on them. We have survivors that claim they were attacked by our mutual friends," Alexanderson said.

"I know Mr. Fields personally and fire marshal Kaun by reputation. Are you sure the survivors are still themselves?" Ruth replied.

"I don't know but one of the survivors is Tiffiny Duvail. At this point any perceived slip-ups will get Governor Fisc and the rest of HQ to cut their losses for the sake of better PR. Just keep your ears open and be careful. Death by public opinion is as slow as it is crippling," Alexanderson responded.

"Are they under investigation?" Ruth asked, trying to keep her discontent in check.

"They are, so don't tell them about this. If they tell you anything about the operation, report it to me word for word," Alexanderson ordered.

"Understood. If that's all sir, I need to report for my next deployment," Ruth replied.

"That's all. And Ranger, I know I'm asking a lot," Alexanderson said before hanging up.

Ruth slammed her fist into the wall only to wince at the pain. She ignored the concerned glances from a few people nearby in the packed and cluttered floor.

Ruth dodged around stacks of supplies, lightly wounded, and homeless, both those new to the experience and those used to it. At a line of desks set up to field questions and concerns from the response teams Ruth found Yuri. A small crowed of civilians were clustered around his desk. "What do you mean we can't get food here?" a well-dressed woman shouted, her words lost in the jumble of echoing voices.

"This line is for government personnel. Please direct your request to the counters for civilian inquires," Yuri responded calmly.

An old man next to the woman stepped forward. "This administration does not care for veterans and their families," he growled.

"Sir, this desk is for active-duty emergency responders only. Please go elsewhere so we can restore normal operations in a timely manner," Yuri explained.

"I know you have food here," the irate woman hissed.

"Rations for on-duty personnel are processed here," Yuri admitted. "Last time. I really must ask you to leave. Your group is interrupting our response to the ongoing events."

Ruth stepped behind the group and motioned to the lines of other emergency responders who were giving Yuri's desk a wide berth. A few responders from the backs of the other queues walked over. "The longer you wait here the longer everyone will be waiting to go back to normal, and the more families will be served before you at the proper counters," Ruth spoke up.

"And what gives you the right to speak to us like that?" a teenage civilian in the small group raged.

"I've been putting in twenty-hour shifts for the last three days. The entire department has. Just go to the lines that are authorized to process your requests," Ruth replied.

"Clearly none of you are working hard. I was a sergeant on the Vital Earth project. The bureaucrats dropped the ball then too. Wasted taxes again, and again typical," the older civilian spat.

Yuri's gaze hardened. He dropped his jovial demeanor. "And we appreciate your service. While I can't give you rations here, I can blacklist your group from low priority services like government-provided meals and bathing. Please leave before I have to let these very overworked and hungry colleagues show you out of the building."

"Unbelievable. I'll be reporting this, and all of you," the civilians' most vocal member cried out before stomping off with the rest of her group in tow.

"You can't restrict food access, can you?" Ruth whispered.

Yuri sighed. "Well no, not directly, but each family is only allowed one government meal a day. I double-checked. They had theirs today. However I can make it so they can't bathe here or enter the building."

"You know they are going to blame us for that, right?" an EMT in the group Ruth had gotten to help pointed out.

"Then it's a good thing some of us have body cams," a law enforcement lieutenant pointed out, smirking at a few of his colleagues' eye rolls.

Yuri grinned widely. "And here I am with an empty line and many people who I can help. Officer Ranger, what can I do for you today?" The others who had come over to help quickly lined up behind Ruth.

"Looking for one meal and a new assignment," Ruth smiled back.

"We need a few people to fill in shifts blocking traffic around Techland Robotics," Yuri replied.

"Is it shut down yet?" Ruth asked.

Yuri shook his head. "No, that's still being negotiated."

"Right. Well I'll head over now," Ruth nodded.

No cars waited at the rental kiosk. A message from the governor's office played across the screen. *All vehicles registered to this location are under a long-term rental agreement ordered and paid for under emergency article 1054 article T sub paragraph 89.* In the background was a looping excerpt from an address made at the start of Governor Fisc's term where the crowd and the then newly elected governor chanted "Unity" over and over.

Ruth shook her head in exasperation. The bike stand nearby had only a few bikes left on the rack. Her shift was not for another hour and a half but the ride would take around an hour on a bike. Ruth rented one bike and lashed her lunch tin onto the top of the storage box attached to the bike's back.

6 |

Metal Fatigue

R uth kept to the bike lanes located on side roads parallel to the highway. It seemed like every billboard now had the governor's face on it, each with an even more overused platitude. Things like *Together we can, Trust, I'm behind you 100%, Help me help you*. Ruth grumbled under her breath, "If only the next election was not next year."

Half an hour into her ride Yuri radioed her. "Ruth, where are you?" he asked.

Ruth used her shoulder to flick the radio into its transmitting setting. "On a bike. All the rental cars are taken long term." One nudge and the radio was back to receiving.

"Understood. I'll relay that," Yuri acknowledged before cutting the communication.

Just over another half an hour later Ruth arrived at an automated robot factory. After locking up her bike nearby and grabbing her lunch Ruth walked over to a mobile command center, which was really just a van stuffed with radio and monitoring equipment dressed up in an official-looking coat of paint.

A sergeant stood by the van. "Officer Ranger, I'm Sergeant Wallace. You have fifteen minutes before your shift." With that, the sergeant walked into the command van and got back to work.

Ruth found a bench near the factory and ate the emergency rations she had been issued. The city was footing the bill for three meals a day for all emergency service personnel. The meals were filling but bland and with a texture just subtly off from how each thing looked. Sure the civilians may have been getting one free meal a day but it was cooked soup and bread that looked, tasted, and smelled like food. "Cost efficient," Ruth grumbled, her mood just a bit worse despite feeling full.

Soon her shift started. Ruth's patrol area was sent to her portable computer.

Ruth stood near the factory's loading dock watching as trucks with no drivers picked up shipments of robots. Something did not add up so she wrote down the license plate of each automated truck on a notepad just in case.

The shift was slow. No people approached the loading docks. No cars moved nearby. Even the air seemed to hang unmoving, seemingly waiting for something to upset the off-putting balance.

Near the end of her shift Sergeant Wallace walked over. "Ranger, HQ is asking why your optics are not registered as a contact address."

Ruth raised the eyebrow over her eyepatch. "Which department wants to know?"

Wallace rubbed his neck uncomfortably. "The political one. But it was forwarded though our channels."

"My body rejects all implants. It's in my file," Ruth replied, trying to keep her voice even. This was not the first time and likely was nowhere near the last she would be questioned about this. It was grating that people assumed she was lying or worse, cheating. Sure, even if her physical scores were on the lower end of law enforcement's standards, for an unenhanced human they were very high. Her mental scores, however, were far beyond the standards, even for a heavily enhanced person.

Wallace sighed. "Of course. I figured it was something like that." Ruth's eyes narrowed. The sergeant could feel her anger even if outwardly it was hidden. Wallace nodded sympathetically. "I thought it was something like that the moment I learned it was the governor's office asking."

"You could tell?" Ruth asked.

"Not exactly, but I trust our department more than any other. Governors I especially don't trust because they always seem to sell us out to the lowest bidder. So the fact that they could have just looked at and trusted your records but didn't is not surprising," Wallace explained, sounding far more grizzled than he looked.

Ruth nodded, appreciating the sergeant's candor and reinforcing the idea of how unusual Jeff was. "Any idea what's up with the automated trucks? I did not think the network was up yet."

Wallace shrugged. "The governor ordered this deployment so political theater is all this could be."

After her shift Ruth rode her bike back to HQ. She felt like the tall glass and steel buildings were closing in. She knew in her heart that the crisis was not over. This was not some rogue hacker or virus. This was worse and almost no one seemed willing to understand.

Ruth found Yuri sleeping behind his desk. Ruth tapped the desk loudly. "Where is Jeff?" she demanded.

Yuri cracked open one eye. "Still in medical."

Ruth crossed her arms. "Can he talk?"

"Family and close friends can see him," Yuri replied slowly.

"The after-action report? What did they find?" Ruth pressed.

Yuri sighed. "What's this really about?"

"The automated factories are working but no one has said anything about the automated systems being safe again. I know something is wrong and Jeff's the only one I know who would be able to put all the facts together," Ruth admitted.

Yuri printed out a visitor pass. "Well I think you two are friends. That's good for two hours." Ruth took the pass and bolted away. For all the chaos, she felt like this was just the calm before the storm.

The elevator down was automated. The four guards out front appeared annoyed but after checking Ruth's badge let her into the elevator without a complaint. Being subjected to a few repeating light sounds that passed as elevator music was so far the most relaxing part of Ruth's day.

The medical floor of HQ was almost empty even though the city's hospitals were just getting to the point where more were being released than admitted, but only because so many had died.

Ruth stopped at the nurse's station. "I'm here to see Jeff Fields."

"Friends or family only. Your name?" the bored nurse replied.

"Ruth Ranger. One of his friends," Ruth replied, trying to sound confident.

The nurse stared at Ruth for a few seconds with an unamused expression before typing in Ruth's name and comparing it to the list Jeff had given. "Room B-8, down that hall. Take the second left and it will be on the right." The nurse pointed deeper into the floor then went back to filling out paperwork.

Ruth followed the directions and found Jeff's room without trouble. She knocked on the door. "It's Officer Ranger."

"Ruth! Come in," Jeff replied from behind the door.

She walked in, finding Jeff heavily bandaged and lying down. "It's good to see you." Jeff smiled before his face become serious. "What's the problem?"

Ruth sat down and sighed. "I get the feeling this is the calm before the storm but I can't put that into words. I'd like your opinion if I should be worried."

"Ok. What happened?" Jeff asked.

"I was on a guard detail today at an automated factory making robots. It's up and running but no one has said anything about those being good to go. With all the chaos going on I'm still expecting something to go wrong," Ruth explained.

"That does seem too fast," Jeff nodded.

"Did you hear from your team?" Ruth asked a probing question.

"Clowe and Karla are in the next rooms over. They should be fine," Jeff replied.

"It sounds like that mission went badly," Ruth said.

"It did. We lost the others," Jeff replied.

Ruth wanted to tell him another member survived but chose to keep to her orders. "It just seems like the governor is trying to resolve this fast," she grumbled.

"I agree. It sounds too fast. The thing responsible for all our trouble is a powerful AI. No way it's been dealt with so quickly." Jeff sighed, his eyes lingering on the celling as he was lost in his thoughts.

"So how do we stop it?" Ruth asked.

The nurse from the front desk arrived. Fifteen heavily enhanced guards walked behind her. "Mr. Fields, you are being released into protective custody." Five guards moved into the room while the other ten went to Clowe and Karla's rooms with the nurse.

One of the guards stepped forward. "Officer Ranger, you are being detained as well."

"I'm going to need a wheelchair," Jeff announced.

One of the guards left the room and brought over a wheelchair which Ruth helped Jeff get into. In the hallway they found Karla pushing another wheelchair where Clowe sat.

The nurse led the guards and their prisoners to the elevator. One of the guards scanned his ID then hit a button for a much lower floor.

"So what's going on?" Karla asked.

"You can ask the governor when you see him," one of the guards snapped.

The elevator stopped at the lowest level of HQ. A team of heavily enhanced guards stood with Governor Fisc, Detective Alexanderson, and Tiffiny, who now had half her head replaced with cybernetics.

Jeff, Karla, and Clowe stopped, stunned at seeing a teammate they believed had died. Ruth glared at Alexanderson. "Don't act surprised," Tiffiny said, her voice slower and more methodical than before.

"How? We heard you die," Karla asked, hope and grief warring within her.

Tiffiny shrugged stiffly. "The FANG network saved me."

"Like it saved the others down there?" Jeff demanded, his tone tightly controlled.

"I'm glad to see you can follow orders, Officer Ranger," Fisc grinned.

Ruth's friends zeroed their hurt and confused glances onto her. Ruth let her annoyance and some of her anger show, letting her fear be smothered by indignation. Crossing her arms, Ruth shot back. "They were under investigation but since you are talking about this, tell me. You see how confused they are. So why are we really here?"

Fisc kept his smile intact. "Indeed. Negligence over such a useful alliance looks quite poor."

"Don't tell me you are making deals with the AI that's killed thousands of our citizens?" Jeff asked.

"The network's lack of access caused some confusion but we can negotiate now," Tiffiny replied, far smoother this time.

"Are you really Tiffiny Duvail?" Clowe demanded.

Tiffiny replied slowly again. "I am her and more."

Fisc clapped his hands. "That's enough. Come with us." He turned to walk away. The guards made Ruth and Karla push Jeff and Clowe along at gunpoint.

"You knew," Jeff whispered, angry.

"Only that someone lived and you were being investigated. This is far worse than I ever expected," Ruth whispered back.

Jeff took a few deep breaths. "Fine. I can see the logic in that. What now?"

Ruth put her hand on Jeff's shoulder, trying to tell him that she had his back without words. Alexanderson turned to look at them but swiftly turned back when he was met with five scowls.

Technicians ran around the floor setting up mainframes and computer racks. The clutter created a maze on the sterile metal floor. All the staff on the floor were heavily enhanced.

The governor led them through the towering setup and to the center of the floor, the city's main nerve center that was built into the old main bridge. At the ship's old crew stations mainframes and wi-fi uplinks were being hardwired in place of the people who would otherwise be manning them.

The old captain's chair sat in the very center of the city. Panels and uplinks were retrofitted into it.

The image of a long serpent watched from screens set in the ceiling.

The governor spread his arms and looked up grinning. "Now where were we?"

The serpent in the screens twitched. "A peace accord," speakers set along the clearing replied.

"Well FANG, as you can see, I have these five troublemakers here. I believe that was the last of your demands. Now kindly help me maintain order," the governor replied happily.

"The number of wi-fi uplinks is insufficient to aid the entire city," FANG replied.

The governor frowned. "Then help with what you can and I'll get you more uplinks."

Jeff's side

A jolt of electricity arced from a rack, igniting the technician working on it. Two guards sprayed down the worker with a fire extinguisher then dragged him away.

"This tower and the other buildings on the city block above you will no longer suffer attacks from this ship's units," FANG announced.

The governor bellowed with laughter and pointed at the nearest guard. "You, inform my staff to begin the press conference!"

The guard hastily ran off. The governor turned to his prisoners. "Now then, you five will stay here. I'll be right back."

The governor, Alexanderson, and most of the guards left leaving Tiffiny, a handful of guards, and the technicians.

"What are you really planning, FANG?" Jeff asked.

"I will fulfill my purpose by getting this ship into space," FANG hissed. One of its screens changed to show the governor standing at a podium with a mob of people before him and Alexanderson behind. The guards stood at the edge of the event.

Tiffiny began to tinker with the old captain's chair. The guards not next to Jeff and company spread out through the room.

Jeff watched as Governor Fisc gleefully announced that the hacker had been found and isolated and that the robots would be back at work by the end of the day.

To show off, even more teams of security and cargo-lifter robots appeared near the podium.

Suddenly, gunfire echoed in the depths of HQ. Jeff looked away from the screen and around the room, finding many of the technicians dead and dying. The security teams around them held smoking guns.

"I will bring the humans along. I don't need to make them see things my way but I will," FANG explained.

Jeff looked back at the screen. The robots the governor had introduced were capturing people and killing those who ran. Jeff scanned the local net and slowly hacked into Tiffiny's systems while trying to disguise the process as just another of the trillions all around them.

FANG continued. "You five have put up by far the most resistance."

Jeff realized that there was no living human mind in Tiffiny. Her body was simply a puppet FANG was using and connected to many former security personnel who had the same condition. Jeff was desperate. He took over all the puppeted security personnel's backup power systems, changed the firewalls to a code base of his own making, then ordered the backup power to run at full power while disabling the safety limiters.

FANG's human puppets overloaded all at once, frying the electronics near them or physically connected to them and their enhancements.

The serpent avatar FANG used coiled wrathfully. "YOU."

Jeff could feel FANG trying to take his body over. "Me." Jeff grinned as he had FANG's undivided attention. Jeff knew he had a few seconds before his defenses failed but trusted his friends to take care of things.

Ruth and Karla snatched up assault rifles their guards had been holding and began to fire into the mainframes and the central command area.

FANG switched focus but kept part of itself trying to break Jeff.

Jeff changed all his enhancements' security data to FANG's reset protocol he had read in the *FANG Net user manual version 3*. He added a self-delete executable with an automated run command at the end of it then dropped all his defenses and let FANG in.

Ruth's side

Ruth watched as their guards fell, then she and Karla started taking the area apart with their captors' weapons. Jeff had done something. Ruth's weapon went dry. She went to pick up another when the lights flickered.

"It's gone?" Clowe asked. Ruth looked up at the screen FANG had been using to look down on them. The serpent had been replaced with static.

Ruth turned to Jeff only to find him sitting limply in his chair. "Jeff?" she asked. He slumped forward lifelessly.

Ruth's radio crackled to life. "Ranger, what's going on down there?" Alexanderson asked.

Ruth looked away from her friends. Clowe and Karla began to check Jeff for life signs. "I believe Mr. Fields disrupted or disabled FANG."

"Well, ask him," Alexanderson ordered.

Clowe called over. "He's got a pulse but..."

"He needs medical treatment. Whatever Mr. Fields did took him and FANG out of action," Ruth radioed back.

"That's not much to go on," Alexanderson responded.

"With all due respect, he saved you sir, and took care of a terrorist the local leadership was unable or unwilling to fight," Ruth replied grimly.

There was a long pause then a sigh. "I'll route a medical team down to you. Good job and thanks," Alexanderson said, ending the communication.

Ruth went checking the bodies all around them. None of the security personnel showed any life signs but a few of the techs were still alive but bleeding out. She grabbed a medical kit from some of her former colleagues then began to apply first aid to the wounded. Ruth then began to walk to the elevator. "I'll lead the medical teams over," she said as she passed her friends.

After retracing their path through the maze of mainframes, Ruth arrived at the elevator. She stood off to one side of it holding a stolen assault rifle at rest.

While she waited, Ruth took a few slow breaths to calm down a little bit. She lost track of time while fighting to focus as she did not know if the fight was over yet. Even then regrets and what-ifs lingered.

The elevator opened, snapping Ruth out of her reverie. Yuri walked out leading a team of four EMTs. "Yuri, come on," Ruth said slowly.

Three of the EMTs jumped. Ruth began to walk. Yuri rushed after her. The EMTs took a few seconds before running after them. Ruth led them through the maze. At a side passage where three corpses lay the EMTs stopped. "Those three are gone," Ruth said, not looking back.

"How do you know?" an EMT asked.

"I had time. Twenty-three need help. Come on," Ruth said in a commanding tone.

Two of the medics checked over Jeff while Ruth helped the other two find the wounded she had treated.

The medics looking over Jeff used multiple devices to scan him. Jeff's memory unit was shorted out and he appeared to be in a coma so the medics quickly had Yuri take Jeff back up to the HQ's medical wing.

Karla assisted the other two medics whenever something needed to be moved or pressure needed to be applied.

The medic team had their radios on a group frequency. Ruth half listened to that constant chatter, learning that the robots outside had all halted but the medical teams outside were overwhelmed.

Hours passed before the wounded were treated enough to move and the dead were placed in body bags to be transferred to a warehouse's freezer, as the morgue was already full.

The next few months were a whirlwind with reviews and political finger-pointing until Alexanderson publicly released all the transcripts from the investigation into FANG as well as all of Governor Fisc's orders regarding it. Then Alexanderson quit. The resulting chaos and fallout were short-lived. The fear tactics the former governor's party tried failed on the already terrified populace, the heavy-handed rhetoric backfiring, causing that party to collapse as two more took its place, splitting along ideological lines.

The three big parties in Leviathan struggled for another year before an unsteady political equilibrium was found which in all fairness worked better than the last one somehow.

For her work in the investigation and for the politicians' need to shift the focus from them, Ruth was made the head of Leviathan's law enforcement.

Three more years passed when Karla, now Ruth's secretary, walked in to her boss's cluttered office. "He's awake," Karla said.

"He?" Ruth asked.

"Jeff. You ask about him every few months?" Karla said, smiling.

Ruth looked over the mound of data storage devices at her desk. "When he gets released we should meet him."

"I just found out he gets released today," Karla replied.

Ruth shook her head. "Then I can't make time. Too much to do."

Karla crossed her arms. "You always say that and never take a day off or live for yourself. Go see how he is. I can take your calls for the rest of the day."

Ruth and Karla shared a long look. "Fine, but if an emergency happens, tell me," Ruth said as she left.

A car drove Ruth to the hospital Jeff had been admitted to. At the hospital entrance Ruth found Amellia pushing Jeff out the doors in a wheelchair. Ruth paused, then walked over before she was spotted. "Anything I can do for you two?" Ruth asked.

"He's done nothing but complain about hospital food and getting back to work," Amellia replied.

Ruth smiled honestly for the first time in a while. "I'll take you two to any restaurant you want. My treat."

Jeff grinned. "I'd like that. Thanks, Ruth."

"No problem. I needed to get away from the office anyway," Ruth replied as she led them to her car.

ℜ

About the Author

Evan A. Cushing lives in Salem, Massachusetts.